HOW WE GOT .

MY HOUSE

My house was the color of silence and dust. Bright things tried to come out in it but they were usually absorbed back into the carpet. The carpet covered the floors and the walls and later my father even decided to glue carpet to the ceiling. He liked the way a good thick carpet could suffocate sounds before they breathed. So he carpeted all the window sills and stuffed wet rags underneath the doors. Outside, the crows scratched their talons on the gutters and squirrels barked in the trees.

HEATING DUCTS

My parents communicated their important messages through the heating ducts. The heating ducts twisted all through the house. They breathed hot whispers into all the rooms. I could put my ear up to the mouth of a duct where it opened in the crack between the wall and my bed, and that way I could listen to my parents. Their voices came through echoed in metal and bent by the heat of the gas. The only parts that made any sense were the parts about the war. I already knew about the war, because I'd learned about it on television.

THE WAR

On television I'd learned that the great nations of the world were building powerful weapons that would keep the world from being destroyed by the powerful weapons they were building, and that after the destruction a cloud would settle over the earth for the next twenty years, everything would be frozen and dark, people would lose all their hair, their skin would melt, and the survivors would live in shelters underground. There wouldn't be any survivors unless you were already underground, or at the bottom of the sea or high in the air, because the flash of light would take away your body and leave nothing but bones. Or not even bones, only shadows. Hair would fall to the ground in clumps and animals would sprout extra heads and the cities of the world would be blown apart until there was nothing but rubble.

SCHOOL

Our teachers never talked about the war. They taught us how to make mannequins. We learned how to paint our own faces on the faces of the mannequins, and how to use the mannequin's head instead of our own head. Our teachers wore skirts that came over their stomachs and their blouses puffed in colors of winds and their hairstyles required whole teams of birds to hover above them and hold them in place. All we ever wanted was to get let out early for lunch, so we threw up our hands and sat with our backs straightened, we organized our pencils on our desks, and practiced keeping our letters between the lines, not letting them slip under or bulge over, and we pledged allegiance to the nation with our hands on our hearts.

PROBLEMS

One day, though, Ms. Thompson fell down, and then Ms. Andrews went blind. No one told us why this had happened. We thought it was probably our fault.

THE FOREST

The forest started in Steven's backyard. His house was at the bottom of a hill, at the end of a dead end street, but actually the forest kept going down, it went down in gullies and mossy ravines, and sprouted mushrooms and clogged itself up with bushes and gave birth to spittle bugs clinging to the leaves. We thought that forest might never stop. Eventually we found out that if you kept going down all the way to the bottom there was a place where the freeway passed over, but we didn't know that yet. So we foraged through the forest for insects, we trapped them in glass jars, and brought them up to Steven's basement, where we poked holes in the tops of the jars and studied the bugs through magnifying glasses. We knew that insects would survive the war, so we wanted to learn how to be more like them.

MY FATHER

When I got home, my father was usually sitting in the kitchen with metal shavings in his hair. For work he drilled holes in things and then put things through the holes. His head got stuck in the machines he worked with and there wasn't much left of him when he was done. He was a kind of mysterious emptiness and gentleness as he sat at the kitchen counter and filled himself up with peanuts and beer. Of course that wasn't true at all. There were all kinds of things inside my father. I knew, because I'd dreamed of them.

THE LEVER

In one dream, my father was trying to pull a lever. He wrapped both hands around it and leaned his whole weight back against it and pulled.

GASH

But he must have pulled too hard or not hard enough because one night we found him in the middle of the kitchen with a big gash in his head. A trickle of blood came from one of his ears and his eyes seemed loose in their sockets. When he came home from the hospital my mother explained that he'd had a reaction. She sat me down in a chair, put her hands on my knees, and said, Your father has had a reaction.

MY MOTHER

My mother knew about reactions. She worked with special children who had reactions all the time. One of them had been struck by lightning and another had bit off his tongue.

AFTERMATH

My father spent some time at home after that. Mostly he sat at the kitchen counter and stared out the window at the neighbors.

THE NEIGHBORS

Our neighbors had decided to keep something awful in their house. From our kitchen we could hear the noises, like the thing was struggling in a flooded basement or thrashing around in the mud. Then glasses would shatter and voices would roar and I'd see Nick sneak out the back, he'd slip through the hole in the fence with some kind of package tucked under his arm, then he'd weave up through the woods and disappear.

NOISES

Later at night, lying in my bed long after dark, when the wind had made its caterpillar nests in the trees, I heard a crackling of branches, and I knew it was Nick coming back to his house, he snuck in through the garage and crept down the stairs and then I could hear that unhappy thrashing coming from the space between the wall and my bed. Our basements must have been connected by some kind of underground tunnel. Water sloshed from one to the other whenever a toilet was flushed. I pulled my bed away from the wall and put my ear right up to the vent and I thought I could hear the breathing of the thing, and the thick wet slap of its skin on the floor when it turned its heavy body over.

MUSHROOMS

Then our school was shut down. In the middle of class we were sent home. My mother told me that mushrooms had grown inside the walls and they could also spread down your throat. So we stayed home for a week while our new school was built.

NEW SCHOOL

The new school was exactly the same as the old one. Only the teachers were different.

THE SWAMP

The most different of all the new teachers was Mr. Yu, who was our teacher. On the first day of Mr. Yu's class he crowded us all into his van and drove us down to the swamp. He gave us shovels and told us to dig in the mud. He said that the mud had swallowed many things and that it was our job to find them. He had a sharp bright bark of a laugh that he added to everything he said. He said that the swamp was once a lake and turtles as big as cars used to lie on its banks and once when he dug very far down he found a sturgeon the size of a submarine. Was it dead? said Steven, but Mr. Yu said no, it wasn't quite dead, nothing was ever really dead, or everything already was, it was hard to tell. So it was sleeping? said Steven, and Mr. Yu laughed and said yes it was sleeping.

WHAT WE FOUND

two rusted cans
a shoe
the skull of a deer
the talking part of a telephone
what might have been an arrowhead
or just a rock
a tire
worms
a dead rat

RIVERS

Meanwhile Steven and I were making our way farther back into the forest. We were trudging down into gullies we hadn't uncovered, gulches carved out by streams that trickled over roots and slippery rocks, and from the high branches of trees we looked out over the forest and saw the parts we hadn't explored, even farther down, where the forest grew thicker and wetter with ferns, where the streams started weaving into one another and the ravines funneled into one big canyon with steep, dripping dark walls, with a fast cold creek running down it, and we hopped along rocks on the banks of the creek and stopped to look into pools, to capture frogs and stash them in our pockets, until one day when it was getting dark and we'd gone down farther than ever we heard a roar, we thought it might be a still bigger river, and so we went on just a little farther and discovered a river of cars.

HUBCAPS

A man named Pete lived under that river in a shack made of scrap wood and metal. He took us down to the burnt forest where the ground was flat and the color of rust and the trees were like scorched ghosts. That was where Pete laid the graves. He had buried people in the roots of the trees and nailed hubcaps to the trunks. The hubcaps looked like mirrors, like round metal mirrors in rooms without walls in a house that went on forever. Did you kill all the people yourself? said Steven, but Pete said no, they'd killed themselves, they'd jumped from the bridge that went over the forest and landed by the creek with a thump. He always dug a few extra graves, he said, for the people who hadn't yet jumped. The graves were threaded with roots running through them and each of the roots bore white wounds where Pete had nicked them with his shovel.

MY UNCLE

My uncle was sitting at the kitchen counter when I got home from the shack. His glasses were so big and thick that he had to keep them from falling down with pieces of string tied to his hat. He wore this little wool hat that made his hair shoot out at the sides and a dark blue shirt that was torn at the elbow. My mother told me that an earlier war had got stuck in his head and now he spent most of his time writing letters to the government. She was always nice and offered him nuts but I knew she was annoyed. He arrived unannounced and talked on and on about radio waves that entered your brain and tape recorders inside the telephone, until my father came home and kissed my mother and hurried him out to the garage.

THE STORM

Then came the storm, which started in the chimney of our house. At first there were just a few shreds of breath, but soon they kindled and caught fire, they snapped and bristled and hissed, and then they shot up and roared out the top and spread their winds through the trees. The spines of the trees shook and their branches twitched with so much fury that some of them snapped and sailed through the sky and landed on the roof of our house. My mother rustled me up from my bed and told me to come downstairs. We huddled in the living room under the blankets and listened to the breath of the invisible animal that had opened its lungs to the sky. The ground groaned, the roots of things trembled. Bullets of rain lashed the windows and flash floods rushed through the gutters. Something cracked and the floor shifted and my father had to crawl under the porch and hold the whole house on his back. I went in to give him coffee,

I crouched there with him for a while, watching the veins in his temples and neck. The storm up above tore at the trees and rattled the windows in their wooden frames while my father knelt with the house on his back and his face held tight like a knuckle.

THE MALL

The next trip we took with Mr. Yu was to the mall. We walked through the high bright halls with the sun shining down through the domed skylights and perfumes wafting from the shops. Mr. Yu took us past all the shops and then led us up the narrow set of stairs that climbed behind the big clock. We went through a little white door and walked down a dim gray hall and we turned left and right and right and left and climbed another set of stairs. Then Mr. Yu went through another door and led us into the museum.

THE MUSEUM OF MASKS

It was a Museum of Masks. The masks were made of thick painted wood. Their mouths and eyes were wide open and they looked ready to scream or eat or laugh, they were laughing and eating animal masks with huge flaring nostrils and teeth, they rushed forward from their places on the walls and stuck their tongues out at us and some of them even had other animals hidden inside their mouths, there was an antelope inside a whale and a beaver in the gullet of a salmon and there were human masks too, huge painted faces with mountains for brows and noses shaped like beaks, bears and foxes coming out of their mouths and those mouths were laughing at us too, all the masks sprang from the walls and jigged and danced and laughed.

MR. YU'S INSTRUCTIONS

We had to look each mask right in the eye and laugh.

THE BASEMENT

In my dream that night I opened the vent and crawled through the duct to Nick's basement. The sturgeon was there, its white webbed fins splayed over the floor and its scales flaking off in places. Its eyes bulged like huge wet globes grown too big for its head. A gray-green glow came from inside it but otherwise the basement was dark. I heard a door open and saw Nick come in and flip open a briefcase and pull out a syringe filled with some kind of liquid. He stuck the needle into the head of the sturgeon and pushed the plunger all the way in and then he sank back against the wall and waited. When its eyes began to close his did too. The gills of the sturgeon opened and closed and Nick's chest rose and fell as water streamed down the stained walls and pooled around our ankles.

BIRD

Then I saw him one afternoon, riding his skateboard in front of our house, swooping around like some kind of bird with the wind always under his wings. He pushed through his turns and kept up his speed and even with his hands stuffed in his pockets he never lost his balance. Turn after turn he zoomed in his circles and carved the street into tight figure-eights until his mother came out onto the porch and tried to call him in for dinner. Then he shot straight down the hill and disappeared.

SPIES

Steven and I started following him. We waited up in my room and when we saw Nick come out of his house we ran downstairs and out the back door and up the bank to the woods. We followed him through the hole in the fence and then we ducked behind some bushes. He sat on a log and started pulling things from his pockets, he wore the kind of pants with the big pockets on the sides, and he pulled out a knife, a box of matches, a roll of twine and some tweezers, a little skull tied to a string and a small leather pouch, a compass, a pocket mirror, dice. He laid these things in a line on the log like he was writing out a sentence. Steven and I studied them and we studied Nick next to them and then we made a decision. If we were going to live through the war, we'd have to be more like him.

POCKETS

So we snuck through the hole he snuck through and collected things like the ones he collected and carried them around in our pockets.

BLUR

Then my father came home one night and buckled me into the front seat of the car and told me we were going on a trip. We raced between rows of billboards and rows of identical trees and the rain thwacked against the windshield. We drove all night and my father's face was quiet. The lights in the rain showed holes in his eyes and there were pits in his skin and places where things were missing. Once we hit a puddle and slid and the cars around us blasted their horns and a bad word slipped from my father's mouth like a thin jet of hot steam.

TORTURE DEVICE

After that trip my father moved out to the garage. He bolted his hands to the sides of his head and stared at the blueprints he'd spread on his bench. He spent all night at the bench drawing blue lines and erasing them, making mountains on the drawings with his brows. The thing he was drawing looked like a spine, a tall metal spine crossed by long metal arms with loops and straps and buckles.

EVOLUTION

The next thing we did with Mr. Yu was watch a film about creatures living in the deepest parts of the ocean. We saw shrimp without eyes and others with eyes on the ends of long tentacles. We saw giant crabs and fish you could see straight through. There were poisonous jellyfish that digested their food outside their bodies, starfish with stomachs inside their arms, and octopi that squeezed their entire bodies into the tiniest crevices. Mr. Yu wanted to teach us that there weren't any limits to what things could be. That was the idea of evolution, he said. He even told us about a special kind of jellyfish that never died. If you stab it enough, he said, all of its cells will just go to sleep, and then after a while they'll wake up, and the same thing can happen again and again. So you keep it from dying by stabbing it? said Steven, and Mr. Yu laughed with his chin in the air and said yes, you keep it from dying by stabbing it.

INCISIONS

In my dream that night Nick went down to the basement and sat with his back against the wall. He opened his briefcase and brought out a knife and rose and went to the sturgeon, with a quick series of stabs and slashes he cut a pattern on its side, a complicated web of fine white lines, and then the sturgeon's eyes flashed open and its fins twitched and its whole body thrashed with such purposeful wrath that the walls cracked and the floor shook and the ceiling began to crumble.

GONE

Then I didn't see him for a while.

LIMP

I saw him once in the woods, lying on a log and staring up through the branches, his long white arms dangling down at his sides like the tentacles of a dead squid.

GONE AGAIN

Then he disappeared again.

WHISPERS

I thought I heard my parents whispering his name through the heating ducts, I put my head down by the vent and listened late at night, and even sat by their door when they were in bed, but their words were hushed and cut off at their ends and suffocated by the thick carpet.

PETE

I went to see Pete. I went down through the forest and found him sitting on the porch of his shack with two stacks of hubcaps at his side. He was picking them up from one stack and wiping them down with a greased rag and then putting them down on the other stack. I told him I was looking for Nick and was wondering if Pete had seen him. I started giving my description of Nick but Pete stood up after just a few words and took me down to the burnt forest and pointed to one of the graves. That's him, he said. I looked down at the grave. Is he dead? I said. Pete nodded and said he was, but then he said that sometimes the people who jumped from the bridge wound up wandering past the burnt forest, they took the trail up beyond the graves to the gasworks hidden in the pines. He pointed a finger up the hill, where the trees thinned out and the ground looked red and stacks of rocks marked a path. That way, he said.

OUR VOYAGE

So Steven and I prepared for a trip. I brought a compass, a pocket knife, and some string, and Steven brought his flashlight and matches. We marched down past Pete and waved to him along the way, we went under the freeway and through the burnt forest and wove between all the graves, and then we followed the little stacks of rocks as the ground began to rise. The trees glowed brighter and the sun shot down through the pine forest in thick and dry dusty shafts, and as we trudged up we heard the squirrels scuttle along the high branches and the crows caw from their hidden perches and somewhere further into the forest a chainsaw chewed through the trees.

THE GASWORKS

The gasworks grew up from the ground like a body without any skin. There were huge rusted pipes that twisted together and connected to other tubes, there were arteries and organs and veins. Everywhere inside and around and up at the top of that big snarled system there were hammocks fattened with the weight of sleeping people and swaying like pods in the wind. Kids down below squatted on the ground and poked whittled sticks into fires. Others were running through the tubes, they popped their heads out and saw us and ducked away, they tip-toed and darted around, and their shouts and cries echoed through the pipes like voices lost from their mouths. I went up to one of the hammocks and looked down at the person inside. He had his eyes closed and his hands folded behind his head and when I asked about Nick his eyes shot open and he blinked at me a few times. If Nick's up here he's probably not interested in being Nick, he said. We don't put much stock in names. If you're looking for names, try going up to the radio tower. There might still be a few names up there. He pointed to a hill where a radio tower rose above the tops of the trees.

ASCENT

The slope was steep and slick with scree and we clawed for a grip with our hands. The trees got smaller and farther apart and then there were no trees at all. We scrambled and slid back and our legs burned and our lungs struggled and our shirts stuck to our backs. Finally the slope smoothed out and breathless we shambled the last stretches and slipped through a slit in an old wire fence and lifted our throbbing heads.

CROWS

But there was nothing much at the top. Only the tower itself staring up at the sky with its blind strivings of metal. And big black birds with lusterless feathers hulked on the dull rusted rungs.

HOT AIR

My father was out in the garage when I got back. The metal spine he'd made from his blueprints lay flat on the ground with a bicycle attached on top. He was pumping his legs and huffing his breath and the garage was hot with his smell.

FOR SALE

A few days later the house next door went up for sale.

HOW WE GOT INTO THIS HOLE

So Steven and I went down to the forest and started digging a hole. We found a tree that had fallen in the storm and in the cavern made by its torn-up roots we dug into the soil. We carved storage spaces into the walls and stocked them with cans of food, we hollowed out alcoves for lanterns and brought down sticks for whittling and dice for throwing and jars for the insects we caught. We thought we might grow shells on our backs and burrow like beetles under the ground and feed on roots and bugs and bark, and we would learn to digest our food outside our stomachs and squeeze ourselves into the tiniest crevices and if somehow the war still got inside us, if the flash of light made our hair fall out or started melting our skin, we'd stab each other again and again.

WATER LINES

1.

When we were in grade school, Bianca and I spent our afternoons hunting for bones. In the forest behind the water tower we dug up the skulls of rabbits and chipmunks and squirrels, and the leg bones and rib bones of other anonymous animals, and we built little mounds of stones for them. The mounds were Bianca's idea and she was also the chief architect; my role was mainly to gather the stones—they had to be white, with fringes of lichen—and she would set them in place, stone upon stone, until the mounds formed small, dome-shaped enclosures. She worked on her knees with a severity of focus that excluded everything else, and she whispered to herself in a language I didn't understand, the words clicking, buzzing, and popping, like insect sounds, like cicadas. Once, when I asked her what she was saying, she looked up at me surprised, her eyes huge and still, and said that she didn't know.

2.

In high school Bianca started calling me in her sleep. My mother would answer the phone, irritated, and tell her please not to call at that hour. I tried to explain that Bianca couldn't help it, she was asleep when she called, it wasn't really her fault, but my mother only frowned and said she should go see a doctor about it. Finally one night I beat her to the phone. Bianca? I said. There was a pause, I heard her breathing, and then in a voice that sounded like it was younger than Bianca's, like she was calling somehow from years before, from the room of a long time ago, she said, Is Alex there? It's me, I said, this is Alex, and then there was another long pause, until she said, I'm looking for Alex. And when I said, Bianca, I'm here, this is me, it's Alex, she paused again and said, Alex? as if she wasn't convinced I was actually the Alex she was looking for.

3.

Though she only lived a few blocks from me, I rarely went over to Bianca's house. She lived in a small house on a tree-lined street with her adoptive parents, whom she called Mother and Father even when talking about them to me, as if they were robots or gods. When I came in with Bianca they would be standing, both of them, by the door, in a kind of formal greeting arrangement, her mother's hair sculpted on her head, her father wearing a forest green cardigan sweater. Bianca would usher me into her room and start rummaging around, looking for whatever it was she had come to collect, throwing things this way and that, kicking things over the floor. The room seemed to irritate her, even anger her, and I would stand to the side and watch the squall of her mood wreak havoc on the havoc that was already there, until she found what she needed and we'd leave out the back. Even when we were outside, walking down the tree-lined street, bits of that squall still whipped at her face like little scraps of black wind.

4.

In the fall semester of her junior year, Bianca was hospitalized for two weeks. No one told me what happened. When I tried to visit her at the hospital, I was blocked by Mother and Father, who stood at the door of her room, their faces gaunt and their lips clamped against their teeth. They said Bianca was going to be fine, but couldn't see anyone at the moment. They thanked me for coming and closed the door. Even when she came back to school, I couldn't understand what had happened to her. She said she woke up one night unable to breathe. She said it was like an animal was stuck in her throat. I thought it was trying to claw its way out, she said. What did the doctors say? I said. A lot of different things, she said, shrugging, and then never talked about it again.

5.

After high school I didn't think about Bianca for a while. I went to college in a different state and only came home very rarely. The floods were already making jobs impossible to find, so after finishing college I moved to a city in the north. I worked at a bakery and lived in a basement room without any heat below a woman whose husband threatened to kill me if I made any noise. One night Bianca called, she said she was in town for a night visiting someone and asked if we could meet at a bar. She had cut her hair very short and looked fashionable in a way that made my own life feel splintered and thin. When we got back to my room, she spent a long time looking at the drawings I'd pinned to my walls. I'd pinned them up never thinking that anyone would ever look at them, and with Bianca's eyes on them now in that cold basement room I felt like I'd been enveloped by some kind of strangeness for years. Eventually we sat on my bed in our jackets and blew warm breaths into our hands and she told me she had to go, there was someone she was supposed to meet.

6.

I saw Bianca again in our old neighborhood. The water line was only a few miles away from my parents' house by then, the power had been out for two weeks, and most of the neighborhood was already empty. On a break from all the packing I took a walk, and wound up on Bianca's street. I didn't expect to see her, but there she was, sitting on her porch with Father, a moving truck outside the house. Father didn't recognize me—Bianca had to introduce me as her old friend—and I'm not sure he recognized much of anything. What I remember about his face was the way a straight white shaft seemed to be striking down through it, starting from somewhere above his head, and striking down through his hairline and through his chin, like a chute through which the remnants of his mind were being emptied. Bianca and I took a walk and talked about our parents and the move and the floods and which northern cities were best. She had let her hair grow out and dyed it blonde, which had changed the shape of her face, or maybe just the way it was framed, and I remember trying not to look at her, trying not to see her but just to listen to her voice, the vaguely distant sound of her voice, as if we weren't walking down the street together but only talking on the phone, as if Bianca had called me in her sleep.

7.

There were those who drowned in the floods, but that didn't account for all the missing people. There were people who left because of the floods but never arrived at their destinations. And there were people who arrived without really making it, people who'd become unstuck from themselves and now wandered the streets of the northern cities with too much white in their eyes, a vacant pulse in their temples. During the winter some of them froze, their bodies contorted on pieces of cardboard, their filthy clothes fringed with grey ice. I was lucky to have found an apartment with heat. I shared it with a woman who had recently arrived from the south. She spent most of her time standing by the window and staring out at the street.

8.

On a rare day when the sun broke through the sheet rock of clouds I ran into Bianca at the park. She was carrying a girl I learned was hers and there was a concreteness to her that seemed new to me and foreign. When she asked what I was up to these days, that question or maybe just the way she'd phrased it seemed to come from a place in her life I'd never visited. I told her about the job I'd found at the library downtown, and she said it was funny, the library was only a few blocks away from the shelter where she worked. I should stop by, they were always looking for volunteers. The whole time we were talking her daughter stared at me with huge dark eyes that knew everything.

9.

In the shelter where Bianca worked I saw a lot of faces shot through with the same white shaft of incomprehension I'd seen in her Father's face, as if they hadn't been able to escape from the floods without the water taking something away from them. I went around to the hunched figures on the edges of beds and asked for names and dates of birth, I asked where people had come from and if they had any medical conditions the shelter should be aware of, and I wrote everything down on the forms Bianca had given me. When people couldn't answer or couldn't talk at all, when they just opened and closed their mouths without any words coming out, their eyes trembling and their lips cracked, I wrote *unknown* in the blank space provided. I took a break at one point and watched Bianca as she hovered in front of those drenched and broken and depleted bodies that seemed randomly scattered around the room despite the order of the beds, as if they'd carried that randomness with them. While she was tending to an elderly woman I thought I heard the words of that other language come stuttering out of her mouth, her throat convulsing with their difficult passage and her eyes widened with surprise, as if her body were startled by this birth of words she hadn't known she was pregnant with. Later when I asked what language she had been speaking, two dark slots opened inside her pupils, and the edges of the room seemed to fold inwards towards us and crumble. Polish, she said. I think it might have been Polish.

10.

A few years later I came across some aerial photos of our flooded neighborhood and sent them in an email to Bianca. I'd been able to identify both of our houses from the shape of the rooftops and the chimneys, and added to the photos little arrows pointing them out. I wrote about how strange it was that the fevered rooms of our adolescence were now underwater, and even stranger that fish were swimming through the spaces where our beds used to be. By that point I'd moved east and farther north and the brutal cold and wind of the winters was getting to me. By contrast to the frozen lakes and windows all around me I imagined the water flooding our houses was warm, and I dreamed about swimming through my old room, enveloped in the eerie, contemplative silence of ruins. I wrote about these things in my message to Bianca, and she wrote back saying thanks for writing and included a photo of her daughter wearing a hat.

11.

I was in a hotel in the mountains when I received the message from Bianca's husband informing me she had passed away. It didn't say when or why or under what circumstances and the note was more of a funeral announcement than a personal message to me. I went out to the balcony and leaned against the railing and felt like a section of my physical substance had been removed, like I was a body with nothing but a box of air where my stomach used to be. I spent the next several days walking the trails. The forest was pristine, everything was glistening, there was an intensity even to the greenness of the leaves that felt menacing and sharp. I kept my eyes on the ground to avoid feeling swarmed by edges, and I looked for animal bones and white rocks with fringes of lichen. When I found a few broken deer bones I built a mound of stones for them. I spent a long time crouched on my knees, placing and replacing the stones, determined to get their arrangement just right, and when it was finally only slightly wrong I whispered some sounds into those stones as if that might fix them in place.

THE SKY AT NIGHT

1.

That summer, I didn't sleep in the same room as my brother. I slept on the porch. I liked waking up in the middle of the night to see if the sky was still there. I was always thinking that someday a sort of garage door might close over it. I'm not sure why.

The summer before, my mother had said we all had to sleep in the same room, so my brother kept waiting for me to fall asleep, or until he thought I'd fallen asleep, so that he could sneak into his girlfriend's bed and slip under the covers.

He was like that snake I'd seen at the zoo. They'd put a rat in its cage, and the snake had swallowed it, until the rat was just a lump inside its body. I'd wondered if that rat-shaped lump was still alive.

I liked sleeping on the porch. I imagined strings strung between the stars. If you could get up there somehow, you could swing your way from star to star. You could move across the whole sky like that, swinging.

The only problem with sleeping on the porch were the ships that passed in the night. They were these huge, slow-moving shadows that made a low grinding noise. I could feel that low grinding noise in my bones. I thought that noise might be the noise of the world, the sound it made on the inside, just grinding and grinding all the time.

2.

In the mornings I met Sophie in our spot, down the beach from my house, where the branches of the trees grew the wrong way. You had to crawl through a thicket to get to the spot, where the light only came through in patches. We would sit in the spot with our legs crossed and plan out our deaths for the day.

Sophie's deaths were much better than mine. She could hold her face in this way that was really dead, her eyelids low and her cheeks flat. I was always stumbling around, my arms out in front of me, like a headless person looking for her head. I was overdoing it, Sophie said. She said that the thing about being dead was that no one could hurt you anymore. It's not all that bad, she said. Watch this, and she would lie on her back on a fallen log, let her long skinny arms dangle down, and close her eyes.

I wanted to learn how to die like that.

Sometimes we would just lie on the beach and stay dead for hours, seeing who could last the longest. I always lost. I was too ticklish. The wind was like fingers on my shins. I'd turn to Sophie and say, How'd you die? and she wouldn't answer for a while, she would just keep lying there, until finally, in a voice that sounded distant, even lost, she would say, My husband killed me on my wedding night.

Those kinds of deaths were the best.

3.

Our house wasn't actually our house. It was just the one we rented every summer. I liked snooping around, looking for things other families had left. I never found much. Some books, a magazine, a comb.

There was one room where none of us slept. We hardly went in there at all. The closet was full of unused pillows and sheets, and the beds were just naked mattresses. We kept the door to that room closed. For some reason we were all ashamed of it.

You could hear everything in that house. It made so much noise, so many creaks and groans, like the floorboards were patients in a hospital. I was the only one who knew which boards didn't hurt. Even in the dark I could move through the house touching only those boards, making mazes on the floor with my feet.

My father was the opposite. He made the house moan more than anyone else. I think he did it on purpose. He was always poking things in their sensitive spots to find out what was wrong with them.

4.

My mother spent her summers standing in the sea. She would stand there for hours, in a broad floppy hat and a shirt that flowed in the wind, the water coming up to her knees. Sometimes her friend from a few houses down would stand with her for a while. Sometimes there would even be three or four mothers. But none of them stood for as long as my mother. My mother stood for longer than all the other mothers combined. Once I'd asked her what she was doing, standing in the water like that all the time. She said it was a little like going to the gas station. It's so your mother doesn't run out of gas, she said.

5.

My brother that summer had decided that everything was pointless. He'd painted his face with a thick paste of gloom that left dark marks in the sink. The music he listened to alone in his room sounded like the low grinding noise.

The summer before, when he'd brought his girlfriend, he'd been a completely different brother. Actually he'd been lots of different brothers at the same time. He kept pinching his girlfriend and trying to hold her hand, and flicking her ears, and teaching her how to tie knots. I felt sorry for her. By the end of the week her face was all rubbery and smudged, like silly putty pressed against newspaper.

I think she dumped him but no one really knows. My brother refused to talk about it. He refused to talk about everything. He spent most of his time with his headphones on, letting the low grinding noise grind into him.

6.

Sophie's house was much different than mine. It was shaped like a shoebox tilted on its end, with windows where walls should have been. The air in it had been scrubbed clean. Her parents stood like herons in the kitchen and stared at things only they could see. Her much older sister floated through the rooms with her hands tucked into the too-long arms of her sweater. Sophie said she was recovering from a mysterious illness. She wasn't allowed to say its name.

Sophie was a different person in her house. She called her parents by their first names and spoke like she had a kind of accent. Her voice sounded like a recording of a voice, like she'd said the same things too many times.

I didn't know how to be in that house. There wasn't any room in it for me.

7.

The summer before, Sophie and I had been thieves. We'd spent our days stealing plums. We knew where to find the best trees, with the ripest and plumpest of plums, the ones that dangled within our reach. Sometimes we snuck into people's yards. Sometimes we climbed over fences. We'd gather the plums in our shirts, then dash back to our spot, where we'd have our plum feasts. Afterword our faces were covered with pulp. Sticky juice ran down our arms. Dizzy with sugar, we'd imagine a world where plums were the only kind of money, where cars would run on plum juice, and the roads would be plum roads, and we'd drive across the country spitting plum pits out of our exhaust pipe. We'd be plum queens. If people tried to tell us what to do, we'd smash plum pies in their faces.

But once we discovered how to play dead, it was all we wanted to do.

8.

My deaths were getting much better. Sophie had told me to loosen my joints, even the little ones, the joints in my fingers, the joints in my toes. Just kind of let them give up, she'd said. I liked the feeling of my joints giving up. I would lie down and let them give up one at a time, until there was just air where my joints used to be. Then all this space would open inside me, and I'd feel like my limbs could almost fall off, like my fingers could suddenly just drop off my hands like dead flowers dropping from their stems. I could stay like that for a long time, my body filling up with the sounds of the sea. When I finally opened my eyes, I'd see Sophie staring down at me, her head slightly tilted to the side. You're getting good, she'd say.

9.

I was glad Sophie liked me again. Last year at school, she'd had a boyfriend, and pretended I didn't exist. She didn't even see me in the halls. She was always walking down a long narrow tunnel with only her boyfriend at the end.

Sometimes I'd seen them sitting together under the stairs, his arm hung around her neck, her head sort of swaddled in his sweater. Her skin looked blotchy and hot. I remembered wondering if she could breathe.

She never told me what happened. All she said was that he turned out to be kind of a jerk. She was much nicer to me after that. We walked home together from school. We're going to steal *so* many plums this summer, she said.

10.

My father thought I was keeping a secret. Whenever I came home from playing with Sophie, he would hover around me in a weird way, shelling nuts and flipping through the paper. He'd keep his eyebrows raised like he was waiting for an answer to a question he hadn't asked. He would breathe in deeply and say, Well? and then just stand there, blinking, like I was supposed to fill in the blank. Usually I would just drink a glass of juice and then walk down to the beach.

When the tide was low, I'd take off my shoes and walk out as far as I could. I liked the feeling of the cool hard mud on my feet. I was always hoping to find something the sea had left behind, a pocket watch, a shark's tooth, a fossil.

You could walk almost anywhere when the tide was that low. Sometimes I'd walk around the point, to the cove next to ours, which was bigger and a little more busy, with an anchorage and a long wooden dock. I'd go out to the end of that dock and stare down at the pilings, where the barnacles clustered and the fish came to feed and the seaweed flowed in and out.

One day when I was sitting like that I met a woman named Ron. She poked her head out of her boat and said, Well hello, and then brought two buckets up from below and set them down on the dock. She had big arms and a round ruddy face with lots of dimples and lines in it. She told me she was going hunting for clams and that I could come along if I wanted. On the beach she gave me a little shovel and pointed to the holes where I should dig. They're down there if you dig deep enough, she said. I liked finding the small heavy clams, their hard halves sealed by the soft living thing. I found a lot. You're a natural, said Ron.

Later Ron hung a sign on her boat and we motored around in the cove, selling clams to the people who were anchored. She said she sold more than usual that day. She said I was good luck. Come back anytime, she said.

11.

My mother was cooking when I got home. Actually she was sort of standing to the side of herself, like she'd made a copy and stepped outside it. Sometimes I thought she wasn't in the kitchen at all. Sometimes I thought she'd split down the middle and slipped away through the gap. Maybe she'd gone back down to the sea so she wouldn't run out of gas.

I wished I could learn how to copy myself. It would have been perfect during dinner, when my father waged a silent battle against my brother. Even my father's little physical tics, like scratching his temple or rubbing his chin, were somehow aimed at my brother. My brother kept his head down, his eyes angled to one side, making hidden comments with his brows.

I'd eat as fast as I could, wash my dishes in the sink, and go out to meet Sophie in the woods.

12.

Our deaths in the woods were different. They were more gloomy and real. In the light of dusk Sophie's face looked like she had frozen to death. Her lips were bloated and blue. You could see the veins in her throat. Are you cold? I would say, and she would pause for a long time before saying, really slowly, I can't remember. She had this way of sucking the marrow from her words so that all you heard were the hollow bones.

We would walk down into a ravine, until the forest flattened out at the bottom, made a little stage, the trees like the columns of ancient ruins. The trails in that part of the forest just wove around through the groves, making circles and figure eights. We'd take different paths, then pretend we couldn't see one another when we crossed. That was Sophie's idea. Dead people can only see the person who murdered them, she said.

She had an eye for the best places to die. She would lie down on a patch of moss and make her hair spill out around her head, so that her skin looked paler than it was, and her hair darker, like seaweed swirling underwater. Or she'd lean against a burnt tree, so that her face glowed against the charred bark. Or she'd drape her body on a narrow log that opened her chest and showed all her ribs. Her deaths looked like paintings to me. They were so ghoulish and good.

One night when she came back to life she sat up a with a kind of glint in her eyes. We should totally get paid for this, she said.

13.

The next time I saw Ron, she gave me a tour of her boat, which was full of things she'd collected in her travels. The inside was like a tiny museum. There were bottles and tins from foreign countries, the dried-out bodies of starfish, a copper hook that had turned green. There was a comb made from the bone of a whale, a rusted chain, a necklace, and a compass. Then there were things I didn't know the names of, things I'd never seen. I felt like I was inside someone else's dream.

It's just a bunch of junk, really, said Ron, and laughed.

We motored across the channel, to an island on the other side, where there weren't any houses. We pulled up on a beach and walked around that island for a while. I asked Ron if she'd always lived in her boat, and she told me she used to be a teacher, but that one day the school where she taught closed. Just like that, open one day, closed the next. You never really know, said Ron.

That was when she'd bought her boat, and now she was making her way up the coast, hopping from island to island, selling oysters and clams along the way. How far are you going? I said, and she said she was heading for the Island of Disappointment, which was famous for its shipwrecks. They say you can find almost anything on the beaches of that island, she said. Anything at all. Gold coins, suits of armor, skulls. You name it, said Ron.

We collected some oysters and then motored back. At the dock Ron said it was time for her to be on her way, since the tide was right. Good luck at school, she said, and winked.

Then she motored off in her boat, waving once before she disappeared from the cove.

I walked home along the road. The sky had that pale yellow color that meant summer was coming to an end. I wondered if my school could just suddenly close. I wondered if things could just stop, or if the low grinding noise underneath everything would always keep pushing them along, basically in the same direction.

14.

Our first public deaths took the island by surprise. We thought a lot about where to stage them, places where people would be shocked, where they'd come around a bend and find Sophie's body splayed over a log, her arms turned so the ghostly skin on their insides showed. She put make-up on that darkened the hollows under her eyes, and did a thing with her lips that made her look especially dead, opening them just a little, like she'd been whispering a secret in someone's ear when she died. She got a few screams and some gasps, and some people just froze, just stood there in shock, and then I'd come around as Sophie bowed and collect money in a hat. Afterwards we'd run laughing back to our spot, count the money and plan our next act.

Mostly it was Sophie who died. I discovered that I didn't actually like being publicly dead. I liked just lying there, my whole body open, for as long as I could, but it didn't work when other people were watching.

Sophie imagined all kinds of deaths. She wanted to do murdered versions of prom queens, cheerleaders, and school presidents. Maybe when we go back to school, she said, we can get costumes. We'll do deaths in the halls and in the locker rooms. We could even do a death at a dance. That would be the best, she said, her whole body humming. It was strange to see that excitement in her when her eyes were still painted dead.

But the best part for me was running back to our spot, almost tripping because we were laughing so hard. That laughing kind of running made me feel like even if a garage door closed over the sky and all the strings between the stars were cut, I could keep running all the time.

Then I'd run home, stash my share of the money in the room we didn't use, and go out to the porch. I'd stare up at the sky. I liked watching the planes. The fading lines they left behind looked like the white wakes of boats.

MOVING OUT

I.

We're coming home from school, walking up the hill, Marco in front, his head down, his hands buried in the pockets of his jeans, Laurel behind him, the collar of her shirt spilling out of her sweater like a tropical plant, then Samantha, agitated, as if struggling to free several birds from the snags in her hair, and finally Peter, our little brother, who lags behind us and sings:

> and all the people said
> what a shame that he's dead

Here's our house, near the top of the hill, a large brooding thing with a few shreds of fog clinging to its heavy eaves. We crowd into the kitchen, where our mother has assembled an enormous array of take-out boxes on the counter. We eat with the silence of animals, while our mother sits at the head of the table and talks on the phone to her friends, her voice branching, multiplying, the strands of it twisting and twining, as she gestures with her glass of wine, with three glasses of wine, with four arms, with too many fingers to count. Eventually she rises and glides up the stairs, still talking, still gesturing with her glass of wine, her voice becoming spidery now, filling the house with intricate, malevolent things.

'Pass the Pad Thai,' says Samantha.
'Pass the spicy beef,' says Peter.
'Pass the prawns,' says Marco.
'There's way too much of everything,' says Laurel.
'You'd rather starve,' says Samantha.
'Laurel wants to be a monk,' says Marco.
'Laurel would make a good nun,' says Samantha.
'Laurel is a moose!' says Peter.
'Peter is a mouse!' says Laurel.
'Can't we ever stop with the games?' says Marco.
'Marco's too old for the games,' says Samantha. 'They're below him.'
'Everything is, we all are,' says Laurel.
'…' says Marco.

Now we go to our rooms. We try to sit at our desks, curl up in the corners of our beds, sink into ourselves, surround ourselves with pillows and books, drape ourselves in blankets and thoughts, but we feel too restless and wrong. Samantha wants to rip off her face. She pushes her fingers into her face and makes it even more awful than it is, this round pale face that contradicts everything she feels. She'll rip it off and grow a new one, a man's face maybe, or an owl's. Peter is flipping through his astronaut book. What he likes is the way the astronauts' heads are encased inside those globes of clear glass. He wishes his own head were encased like that, everything quiet, everything calm. Marco has had enough. He's sick of these voices in his ears, everyone trying to tell him who he is, Marco is this, Marco is that, Marco is above it all. He shuts his door, not slamming it exactly but shutting it hard, and Laurel knows that door is for her. She feels it hit her almost physically. It's as if her body extends into

Marco's room, into all of the rooms of the house. She wishes she could make it contract, with a muscular effort, like an octopus retreating to its crack in the rocks.

Samantha wakes in the middle of the night. She hears, coming from our mother's room, an opening and closing of drawers. Our mother must have hidden something in the dresser, she thinks. Or something has been hidden from her. She closes one drawer and opens another, rummaging through drawer after drawer, her nails scraping the wood paneling at the bottom. There's something furious, something desperate in that scraping, and in the speed of the opening and closing, as if the number of drawers keeps increasing, as if each drawer our mother closes creates three others, as if the whole house is made of drawers, and the hidden thing flits like a particle between them. Mother can't track it down, can't keep up with the crazed pace of that flitting, that fleeting, and she starts to break up, to come apart, losing pieces of herself with each drawer she opens. She goes through them again, in a different order this time, or no order at all, like someone playing wrong notes on the piano, notes in no key. This is the true music of our house, Samantha thinks, as she lies wide awake in her bed. This is its song.

Laurel wakes when our father comes home. She hears the front door open and then his suitcase rolling over the floor. He moves heavily, haltingly, the weight of him creaking through the wood of the house. She imagines a kind of rectangular shape, a pinkish-grey homogenous block, standing in front of the refrigerator. She knows it's not very nice, to think of our father in this way, as a pinkish-grey homogenous block communing deeply with the refrigerator, but she can't help it.

Now she hears him climbing the stairs. It's such a recognizable sound, our father's slow, laborious climbing, so full of fatigue, as he lugs his suitcase from stair to stair. Maybe one night he'll just stop, homogenous block that he is, and be content to spend the rest of his days sitting on the stairs with his suitcase. She'll be the one to sit with him, of course. She'll feel bad for him. She always does.

Peter is woken by the wind rattling his windows. The windows of the house are old, the wood of their sills has withered and shrunk, and the wind knows this, knows how easy it is to sneak into Peter's room, slink up to his bed, and lap at his face with its wet tongues. Frog tongues, Peter thinks, and pulls the covers over his head. He hates this house with all its holes. He wants to live in a much smaller house with rooms only big enough for his own body, rooms the same shape as him, like the case in which he keeps his clarinet. That would be the best kind of room, a fur room molded to his shape, with a door that closed with a nice clean click. Now he gets up to go to the bathroom. He sees light still coming from under Marco's door, and pokes his head in, sees him sitting on the edge of his bed, his shoulders hunched, his elbows resting on his knees.

Marco is waiting. He's been waiting all night, for his mother to stop talking on the phone, for Laurel to stop burrowing into his brain, for Peter to stop poking his head through the door. If everyone would just stop filling the house with themselves, with their feelings, the clanging of hangers in their closets, the glooming of moods through their rooms, he might be able to think. And he needs to be able to think. He needs to figure things out. Who the hell is he, should he go to college or not, should he start medicating his brain, why isn't he more interested in girls, why can't he understand calculus, is he forgetting something, why does he always feel like he's forgetting something? But the house won't let him think. The walls are ill at ease. The floorboards are sensitive and weak. And just when everyone has gone to sleep, and it feels like the night will take the house for itself, smother it in coolness and quietness, calm everything down, and let Marco contemplate his life in silence for a while, he hears a click, the front door opens, his father has come home.

In the morning the night hasn't happened. The night is gone, trampled under by our frenzy of showering and dressing, eating and drinking, making our lunches and brushing our teeth. It will come back, the night, or pieces of it, remnants, but for now it has no place, we're too busy stuffing our backpacks with books, bundling ourselves into our coats, and then we're off down the road, Marco behind us this time, his head down, his hands buried in the pockets of his jeans. We're beginning to feel, at least some of us, the first little kicks and grunts of our futures, the first strivings and musings of our eventual selves, so completely at odds with who we are now. Samantha, when she sits down at her desk in her first class, and feels the heat of other people's eyes on her face, takes out her notebook and starts writing words. She writes 'prowl' and 'nettle' and 'sludge.' She writes 'heckle' and 'knurl.' These will be her words for the day. When she writes them down they become hers. No one else can have them. No one else even knows what they mean. She writes them again and again, her handwriting getting a little smaller each time, more contorted, her pen pushing firmly into the paper, as if she's shaping herself with the shapes of these words, printing herself on the page.

Marco keeps hearing his name. Maybe it has something to do with who he is, or maybe it's just the name itself, a sound people like to make, but in any case he hears it everywhere, it echoes through the classrooms and halls, and by lunchtime already there are too many Marcos in his brain, each with a different intonation, a different tone, but all of them pointing to him, all expecting him to answer them, to be Marco in exactly that way, whatever that is, Marco doesn't know, he leaves school after lunch because he says he has a migraine and maybe he does, maybe this is what a migraine is, having too many Marcos in your brain. He goes to the park. He sits on a bench, and starts strategizing ways to get rid of Marco for good, to pull the plug on Marco once and for all. Of course he could always just hang himself. That would be the easiest way. Where's Marco? people would say.

Laurel would actually like to be learning about rocks. She likes this class, likes the teacher, and feels like a break from the world of sentient beings is exactly what she needs. But something in her won't let her have it. She knows Marco left school. She saw him twice in the halls, saw him wincing his way past people, flinching every time someone said his name, and now she feels the tendrils of her sympathy unfurling towards him, reaching out to him, despite her best efforts to coil them in. She hates them, these sticky, untrustworthy things, which always unfurl precisely towards the people who wound her. She wonders why that is. She wonders what made her this way. They're not really *hers*, it's like they've been seeded in her by something else, a conspiracy of biology and patriarchy. And what would happen if one day she decided to cut them off? What would be left of her then? Would there be anything at all?

We hardly recognize Peter. When we come to pick him up after school, he's wearing a hat we've never seen, and he's sitting with his back against a wall, elbows resting on his knees, looking like a page boy from the previous century. His fidgetings, the anxiety that lives in the corners of his eyes, have been chased away by the hat. 'Where's Marco?' he says, and when Laurel says, 'He went home sick,' Peter says, 'Oh.' We start walking home. He deflects all questions as to how he came by the hat. He shrugs. He says he doesn't know. We look at him, peer into him, listen for the stream of his thoughts. There's nothing. It's all hidden under the hat. We walk up the road, Peter in front of us, not singing songs about death, not plugging his ears when ambulances pass, just walking slowly, pensively, as if time has sped up since we left him this morning, and he's no longer the Peter we know.

II

Marco is the first of us to leave. He goes to college in the east and tells the new people he meets that deciding to hang himself was the best decision he ever made in his life. 'You have to live your life as a dead person,' he says. He graduates with a degree in philosophy and on a trip to Europe he meets an older French woman whose husband died in a boating accident. She says his name in a way that embalms his brain by injecting a kind of cool fluid into it, and soon he's moved into her apartment in Nantes, where he spends his mornings in her bathtub, drowning his thoughts, clipping his nails. In the afternoons, while wandering the streets, he learns that by staring at patterns of cobblestones he can lull himself into a hypnotic state in which time ceases its forward movement and spreads out around him instead, a sea of time in which buildings sway with the slowness of things underwater. One day, while looking for a belt in the woman's closet, he discovers that the new clothes she's given him are in fact the old clothes of her dead husband, though Marco isn't alarmed or even terribly surprised by this. In fact his letters from this period are some of the most beautiful he's ever written, full of long, lyrical sentences about the generosity of putting his own self aside, making space for the spirit of the woman's dead husband, so that she can say goodbye, make love to him one last time. Of course these letters sound nothing at all like the Marco we know, and so we're not surprised when, a month later, he comes home, skeletal, fanatical, with a wild beard and a face that looks like a cave. He eats only toast and speaks in a low murmuring tone that's impossible to understand, and our father stares at him with an expression so stark in its refusal to recognize this person as his son that it resembles a kind of peace. Our mother on the other hand wants to call an ambulance. Luckily he leaves before she does. We don't hear from him for months. Eventually he sends photos of himself with his new girlfriend and their dogs, and he's almost unrecognizable, clean-shaven, muscular, tan. We can only imagine that his girlfriend, who we learn works as a nutritionist, has performed a kind of exorcism on him, evicting from his body and brain all the manic and melancholy and anxiety-ridden Marcos and feeding into being this new, gregarious Marco who takes his dogs on long walks and talks about starting a business. We can't quite manage to be happy for him. When he brings his girlfriend to our house for the first time, we're appalled by the blithe aggression of her normalcy, by the way she bulldozes through our fragile family with her platitudes, and above all by the fact that Peter not only tolerates her behavior but encourages it, smiling and laughing at everything she says. A few months after they get engaged Laurel begins receiving letters from him, the most earnest letters he's ever sent. He's been waking recently in a sweat, unaccountable images have been surging into his mind, horrible images, bloody masses of meat and bone, eyeballs shot through with nails, and yet he's happy, he's never been so happy in his life, there's a radiance to things that's almost too bright, everything is splitting open at the seams, like fruit so ripe it bursts through its peel. He breaks off the engagement. After that we receive a few scattered messages, sent from different places, shreds of sentences without punctuation, words that aren't even words, Marco hurtling through the atmosphere like a disintegrating comet.

Laurel has a dream in her last year of college. In her dream she's lying on a beach. Hundreds of crabs emerge from the sea and begin detaching small parts of her body with the voracious efficiency of their pincers. They take the bits of her back to their hiding places under the rocks, where they devour her in private, mutilating her flesh with their greedy mouths. She wakes from the dream feeling exhausted, as if the fibers of her muscles have all turned to pulp. The feeling doesn't go away, she drags herself through her final semester and when she graduates she moves to a small town a few hours south down the coast. She finds a job at a nursery. On her days off she walks along the coast, reflecting on her life, her decisions, her relationships. Loving seems like such a simple thing to her and yet somehow everyone makes a mess of it, everyone mutilates it, maybe she does as well. Convinced she prefers the company of plants, she fills the cottage she rents with an enormous assortment of them, plants in the bathroom and by her bed, the tendrils of plants crawling over her kitchen table, spider plants hanging from her ceiling. When she thinks about the future she imagines starting a hospice somewhere in a remote location where she'll help people die in rooms full of plants. She can see herself walking between the beds, moistening lips and watering plants. There has to be, she thinks, towards the end of our lives, a simplification, a reduction. There has to come a time when the starkness of death brings everything else into relief, and loving becomes the simple thing that it always has been. Gradually she feels the vernal world of her private cottage restoring to her body and her embittered brain the vitality people have sapped from her. It's around this time that our mother begins leaving long, scattered voice mail messages in which she intimates in increasingly unsubtle tones that Laurel has to come home. Everything is slipping away from her, she says, our father is ill and hardly gets up from the couch, he just stares at the empty spaces of rooms, and she hasn't heard from Marco in months, she thinks he might need help, and Samantha is so curt with her, she won't tell her anything about her life, Peter is a darling of course but she doesn't understand him at all. Laurel comes home for a weekend and is alarmed by the state of the house, the refrigerator stinking with rotting things and dishes encrusted with the remnants of meals in a towering heap in the sink. She spends most of the weekend washing and sweeping and mopping and dusting while clots of our mother's harried words reclutter the spaces she clears. After several more of these weekends she gives up, she gives in, she quits her job and moves home, though she keeps paying rent for the cottage and has a colleague at the nursery take care of her plants. At night, when our mother has retreated upstairs, Laurel sits with our father in the living room. For the most part he seems resigned to his condition, which worsens a little every day, and Laurel feels almost grateful to him, assuaged by him, as if he's giving her something she needs. But occasionally something startles him from his sleep, a thought or the beginning of a dream, and his eyes flash open, the whites of them suddenly gleaming and big, and he looks around, without moving his neck, just his eyes shifting, jerking, as if they're horrified to find themselves stuck in his head. Laurel touches his arm, to remind him where he is, that she's there with him, and his eyes soften and settle back into their sockets. But she's left with the memory of those other eyes and knows they can always come again.

In her first year of college, at a party her roommate drags her to, Samantha looks around at the lurching world of sweat and breath and says, to no one in particular, 'None of this is real.' Over the next few years she'll find herself saying this again and again, mostly to herself, sometimes out loud. When she graduates she moves into a house with six other people and finds a job at a bookstore. In her attic room, at a desk in front of the little window that looks out over the city, she writes scraps of things, descriptions, the beginnings of stories, dreams. There's a feeling of concreteness, of precision; even if her sentences are broken and bent, even if they're frayed at the edges, they have the brokenness, the frailty, of reality. Her housemates are vague, spectral presences that drift without purpose from room to room until she presses them into a sentence. The changed thing is the real thing, the definite thing; everything else is forgettable. At the bookstore she meets a person named Julian with painted nails and furtive eyes, slender wrists and accentuated temples. When she writes him down she has the feeling she's missing something and so she sees him again, and again, and there's always more to write down. There is, she realizes, the possibility of too much reality. He is gentle but also intelligent, funny and mysterious and strange, and serious, and playful, with jittery brows and flecks of light that dance in the centers of his pupils. She feels a loosening somewhere inside her, an unbinding; parts of her start spilling out, and she can't regather them all; she stoops down to pick one up and others tumble from her arms. Without intending to she begins identifying, with a kind of anatomical precision, his soft spots. She needles them, probes them, wounds him and then mocks him for reacting to something so small, so trivial. When eventually he limps away to lick his wounds she becomes furious with herself and begins making notches on her arms, carving her fury into her skin. She quits her job at the bookstore, finds work as an editor at a magazine, and moves into her own apartment. She works mostly from home, cutting and manipulating other people's sentences until they have the concision she demands. In her own writing she becomes increasingly fascinated with broken bodies and the ways they can be soldered back together. She writes a story about a woman who wires shut her jaw. She writes a story about a man whose limbs are held together with string. The first of these stories stirs up controversy and suddenly people are saying and writing her name, attributing meanings to her she didn't mean, peeling up the words she'd pinned to the page. Now those words flutter around her with the directionless frenzy of moths. She wishes she'd kept the story in her desk, where she keeps the rest of her stories. She stops going outside, and when we see her, for the first time in a year, at our father's funeral, we're startled by her stillness and pallor, as if she's hidden behind a portrait of herself, retreated behind her own eyes.

From the moment Peter appears in his hat, he's lost to us, like a radio station we used to listen to that's suddenly gone from the dial. And yet, in a strange way, he stays more in touch than any of us. He calls all the time. He just wants to check in he says, see how we're doing, say hi. The sound of his filtered voice on the phone becomes the sound of the new Peter. We can't fathom him. We can't make the link between the Peter we knew, febrile and hounded by fears, and this new, agreeable, eupeptic Peter. We know that he finds some kind of job that involves sitting in a room with other people and having ideas about things. He sends us photos of himself on his boss's boat, which he helps sail down to Mexico, and we see him pictured standing on the bow in the calm brilliant water of Baja, his blond hair swept across his brow. But this isn't Peter. The old Peter must still be in him somewhere, tied up and gagged in some secret basement in the new Peter's brain. When he comes home for holidays, he plays host, takes everyone's order for take-out, makes the calls, gives back rubs, fills the gloomy, potentially volatile silences with his insatiable chatter. But we're all thinking the same thing. Where's Peter? When he sees Marco in one of his low moments, muttering incomprehensibly from behind his wild beard, he sits down with him and talks about things that might help, exercise and regular massages, skydiving and swimming in the sea. He seems completely impervious to the way Marco looks at him from the lost rooms in his brain. Even in those lost rooms we know where Marco is. Not Peter. Peter is promoted and develops a passion for real estate, he amasses properties, investing, speculating, purchasing houses and apartments he's never even seen. There's a zeal in him now, an almost evangelical fervor, he's always on the phone, always taking calls, always putting someone on hold. He weeps copiously at our father's funeral and thanks everyone for coming, giving them hugs, telling them how much it means. We can't quite believe this is real. Marco gets angry when we voice our doubts, he tells us to let Peter be, we keep hitching him to his former self, which was miserable, we should remember, which was always singing songs about death, that's apparently what we want for Peter, to sing songs about death all his life, because the suffering Peter has to be the real one, suffering is always real, isn't it, happiness is always a lie, isn't it, so let's bring back the other Peter, please give us back the miserable Peter full of forebodings of doom, that's the real Peter, that's the only Peter Peter can be. 'So you think this is really him?' says Laurel. 'I don't think anyone is really anyone,' says Marco. Maybe he's right. Laurel remembers the deranged look in our father's eyes and she's just had to give up her cottage, the one thing that was really hers, and our mother is gradually ceding ground to the thicket of her most vicious thoughts. She thinks Samantha is trying to poison her. She thinks Peter is plotting to take her out of the house and lock her away in a tidy little box. 'It's called a condominium, mom,' says Laurel. 'It's called a tomb,' says our mother.

III

We've just had lunch with our mother, at her new condominium, and we're walking up the hill, Peter in front, talking on the phone, gesturing emphatically with his arms, Samantha behind him, her hand clasped like an iron claw to the neck of her coat, then Laurel, the collar of her shirt drooping out of her sweater like an unwatered plant, and finally Marco, lagging behind us, his face hidden by straggles of hair.

We pack boxes. We thought there wasn't much left to do, we thought we'd be done in an hour or two, but we've grossly underestimated the house's capacity to conceal more things in its crevices. We make piles for the dump, piles for the Salvation Army, piles for the children of the future. Marco wants to throw everything out, he doesn't discriminate, doesn't discern, and Laurel has to go around rescuing things from his ruthlessness, salvaging things from his gloom, until she realizes, no, he's right, he's actually right, and starts jettisoning everything as well. It's Samantha who slows us down, Samantha who keeps getting stuck on things, lost in them, sitting down and flipping through yearbooks, finding art projects from junior high, photo albums, cassette tapes, journals. Peter is nowhere to be seen.

He appears later with too much food. Samantha goes out and buys three bottles of wine. We pour it into plastic cups. We eat with plastic forks and knives. We feel depleted. Even eating is somehow exhausting. 'Pass the dumplings,' we mumble. 'Pass the fried rice.' 'Pass the rolls.' 'You can almost hear the echo of the food,' says Laurel. 'You can almost hear our mother on the phone,' says Samantha. 'This is such a beautiful house,' says Peter. 'Such a beautiful corpse,' says Marco. 'Pass the bones,' says Samantha.

We go up to our rooms. Marco flips through Peter's old astronaut book, the one thing he's secretly saved, and drifts off to sleep with those weightless bodies floating through the ether in his brain. Samantha is reading one of her earliest journals. She's appalled by the loops and lobes of her adolescent handwriting, but there's something in the words she recognizes, something in the sound of them, already a rasp, already a snort and a cackle.

Laurel feels herself peeling away from these floors, these walls, these windows, those trees. As for Peter, who knows. He's probably not in his room at all. He's probably already elsewhere, he's flying, he's soaring, he's on his way to the moon.

ONE OF US
WILL ALWAYS BE HERE

I.

And then one summer I drove north across the border to stay for a week in the empty room my friend Viv had written about. I remember the road stretching straight as an airstrip for miles and miles, walls of trees on both sides. I remember seeing Viv for the first time in years and thinking she had something of that road in her eyes, a look I couldn't reach the end of. She was more regal now with silver in her hair and an animal alertness in her temples. We sat on her porch in a dusk that wouldn't end and talked around the edges of our lives, as if our lives were lakes we didn't want to wade into. Later she showed me the room, which was exactly as I'd imagined it, with warped wooden floors and thick ceiling beams and a window that looked out upon a forest. My sleep that first night in the room was a strange light sleep in which I was always vaguely aware, or dreaming that I was aware, that Viv was still awake and watching me, looking for some buried thing in my mind.

In the morning we went for a drive. A man named Tobias picked us up in his truck. We squeezed together in the front seat and drove along a road that was just like the road I'd driven to get here, the same monotony of identical trees. We were on our way to an abandoned house Tobias was using for a film. He'd installed cameras in the rooms that filmed the house day and night. The house had an incredible atmosphere, he said, the most incredible atmosphere he'd ever seen, the lives of the people who'd lived there were almost palpable. His fingers danced on the steering wheel as he talked. Viv sat quietly and stared straight ahead as if she wasn't listening to him but to the effect he was having on me.

We turned onto a gravel road that wove its way towards the coast. The house stood alone behind the line of trees a few hundred feet from the shore. We picked our way across the porch, then entered through a door to the living room, with a couch that looked like the carcass of a cow and a broad black stain in the hearth. Objects were scattered everywhere, bedding strewn on the kitchen table, dishes broken on the living room floor, as if an animal or some kind of internal storm had torn its way through the house. I walked around, careful not to touch anything, aware that I was on film. Then Viv took my arm and led me upstairs to a small attic room with a round window that peered through the trees at the sea. Below that window was a wooden desk with candle wax dripping down its legs. Remind you of anything? she said, as we watched the waves throw capes of spray against the rocks. Yes, I said, my own hot blood now beating on the walls of my brain.

II.

We'd spent a week together in a house like this years ago, the summer before we went off to college and then gradually drifted apart. I'd only known Viv for a year, she'd transferred into my high school as a senior, under circumstances she hinted at but never explained. She was brash, arrogant, erratic. I was the timid bookish girl with an ocean of loathing for everything. We made a pair, awkward and asymmetrical, like a planet in orbit around its own moon.

We slept that summer in an upstairs room with two single beds and a window. At night we'd keep the window open and let the cool sea breezes with their rich smells waft over our restless skin. When I first got there we talked about the things we'd always talked about, books we'd read and films we'd seen and the horrible fates we wished upon the people we hated. But eventually Viv started talking about a man she'd met, not a clumsy boy like the ones we made out with but a man, she pulled her bed closer to mine and described with an iridescent gleam in her eyes what he did to her and wanted her to do, the crazy things he said to her, and how intoxicating it was, to make a grown man say those things, to make a grown man want those things. She felt him coming apart. She felt the locks on all his doors splitting open. He says he's never been like this with anyone else, she said. He doesn't even recognize the person he becomes when he's with me. It's *insane* to feel what's actually inside people. You'll see, she said. He's coming later. I invited him.

I remember the room filling up with spongy heat as she talked, and I remember wanting to put my hand in her mouth to stop her words from flooding the house, but instead I pulled myself closer.

Now we were looking out the window at the sea. The sky was turbid and cloud-strewn. We were quiet and our arms were touching and I sensed that she was watching my thoughts.

III.

Later we watched some of the footage. We sat on the couch as we'd sat in the car, Viv squashed between Tobias and me. Almost nothing happened on the screen, we saw the curtains flutter once or twice, there was the sound of the waves thrumming on the beach and, beneath that sound, an irregular scurrying of mice. For a second a ray of sunlight woke up the cracks in the dilapidated wood, and the whole house glowed with demented glee. Then as the day turned into dusk the forms of things blended together into a grayish, undifferentiated porridge. Weirdly I continued to watch, even when Viv and Tobias went to bed I stayed there riveted to the screen, tensed and clutching my clavicles, like a child waiting for the monster to appear in a horror film.

That night I dreamed of a crime. In the dream we were standing in the abandoned house, Viv, Tobias, and me. The curtains on the windows were flapping in the wind and we were looking down at a pool of blood on the floor. One of us was the killer and one was dead and we were trying to figure out who was who, but someone had to be lying. One of us was actually a wolf. One of us was concealing a wound. It's you, said Viv, in a whispered voice that came from inside my head, and I said, Which one? and then woke with the feeling that I'd never been asleep.

IV.

The next night I went to Viv's bar. On our walk that morning she'd told me how everything had clicked the moment she'd seen it, the parts of her life had snapped together, within a month she'd bought it with her friend Kim and moved her whole life across the border. Kim had short dark hair and eyebrows that angled towards one another like an owl's. I've heard a lot about you, she said when I came in. Not all of it bad. I laughed and sipped a whiskey and soda and wondered what Viv had said.

Tobias came in a while later. After chatting with Kim for a few minutes he claimed the stool next to mine. This place was actually a brothel during the Gold Rush, he said. Then it was empty for years. You should have seen it when we first got here. It was full of rats and garbage and the ceiling was rotting. As he talked I found myself looking at him closely for the first time, noticing his muscular arms, his yellowish teeth, the watery glint in his eyes.

The bar began to fill up. Viv and Kim slid across one another, exchanging a commentary of coded glances as different people came in, most of them men who assumed their stools with a kind of proprietary heaviness. I felt the air around me thicken. Whenever I glanced down at my drink it was magically full to the rim. I asked Tobias about his film, what he was planning to do with the footage, and when he shrugged and said he wasn't sure yet I said, Just keep it the way it is, it's good as it is. He laughed and I said, No, I'm serious, it's perfect, it's the scariest thing I've ever seen, and then I got up to go to the bathroom and must have turned the wrong way when I came out, because I found myself in another room, low-lit and crowded with men sliding packages over a table, a metallic taste in the air.

Later I was sitting on Viv's porch, drunk and watching the sky change colors. I saw her walking home and thought something was wrong with her walk, she had a limp or a hitch in her hip. You disappeared, she said, stepping up on the porch. Old habit of mine, I said.

V.

On our drive the next day to a village on the coast Viv asked me if I was seeing anyone. The question seemed to come from the center of a silence that had been expanding ever since I arrived, opening gaps for the night to rush into. I said no, it had been a while since I'd seen anyone really, and while saying this I felt all the speechless years hovering between us like ghosts. I stared out the window, imagining that somewhere in the forests of the future we were weaving between the identical trees, our faces featureless, amnesiac.

At the coast we walked out to a pier where fisherman were unloading their boats. We sat down and let our legs dangle over the dock. I watched a man pick up a crate of shrimp and suddenly remembered the dream I'd had the night before, Viv limping from room to room in the dark back space of her bar, quietly calling my name. I stopped sleeping with men, I said, taking up a thread that wasn't really there. Viv nodded with her hands beneath her knees and said, Probably smart.

VI.

Later that day I came back from a walk and found Tobias drunk on the porch. He tried to stand up when he saw me coming but instead he only slid back down to the place where his body was slumped. His features were struggling to stay on his face and his limbs swam in their sockets. I wouldn't, he said, when I went in to get him some water.

I went upstairs and lay on the bed. The day felt like it should have been over but the sun was still hovering like a maniacal eye high above the horizon. I got up and started looking around, wanting to know who had lived in this room before me. I found a pair of muddy boots in the closet. I found a fishing reel, a deck of cards, a tape recorder, tweezers. The photographs were in the most obvious place, in the top drawer of a dresser I hadn't used. There were pictures of Viv moving into her house and Viv and Kim working on the bar and there were also pictures of me, of me and Viv in the cabin that summer, sunburnt in our swimsuits and standing on the shore, our arms wrapped around one another, one of Viv planting a kiss on my cheek while casting an eye towards the camera. We looked happy, radiant even, intimate, though now that I looked a little more closely I thought that intimacy was forced, we were putting it on, it was a pose, for the camera or the man behind it, and then it struck me, my thoughts flared, the nerves in my face flashed with heat. The man behind the camera. Him.

VII.

I sat on the porch that night and waited for Viv to come home. When I think back on that week it seems to me now that I was always sitting on the porch, always waiting for Viv to come home. There was a rocking chair where I sat. The creaking sound made by the wood counted the time of the night, which wasn't really time but just a repetition within a dead chunk of dusk. At some point Viv would come around the corner and walk down the street towards the house, limping or concealing her limp. In my memory her outline is blurred, Viv limping has been overlaid with the Viv who concealed her limp. I don't remember which one it was that turned the corner that night. Half of her face looked tired. She sat down on the bench next to me and lit a cigarette. I found the pictures of us, I said, and heard the sentence hang in the air. Viv smiled. She leaned her head back and blew out some smoke. They're cute, aren't they, she said. Yes, I said, and watched a few bats cut slits in the sky and then stitch them up again. Do you remember him? I said, and she frowned a little, still with a quizzical smile on her lips, and said, Of course. She chuckled. I realized now she was drunk. I can't see his face, I said. There's a hole in my memory where his face should be. Viv looked away, her gaze vacating the space between us. You're not missing much, she said, shrugging. And then after a pause she let her arm drop languidly away from her body and swirled the hand that held her cigarette and said, Wild times.

VIII.

Tobias came over in the morning to show us some footage. You have to see this, he said, popping in the tape and sitting down in the middle of the couch. Leaning forward, elbows perched on his impatient knees, he kept looking back at us over his shoulder, twisting and fidgeting, sniffling and scratching his neck. Come on, he said. Viv and I were sitting at the kitchen table. We'd been sitting there for hours, staring at one another over the rims of our coffee cups, testing out a new kind of silence. He's been up all night, Viv said now, quietly, her eyes low-lidded and weary. We got up and went into the living room, sat down on either side of Tobias, and fixed our eyes on the screen. He started fast-forwarding the tape. The abandoned house on high speed seemed to turn something over in its mind, digesting something it couldn't digest. Then he slowed it down, and we heard footsteps on the porch, a stumbling and jostling of drunken bodies as they broke through the door. There were six or eight or seventeen limbs tangling together in the wasted space of the house. Moans came from somewhere offscreen and grunts seemed to heave from the backs of thousands of throats. Then just darkness and breath, the bodies collapsed below the eye of the camera. I knew that Viv was still watching closely, and I imagined the point where my line of sight met hers, just behind the surface of the screen, in the space the bodies had vacated.

Incredible, isn't it? said Tobias chewing his nails.
The other stuff was better, I said.

IX.

You should stay another week, said Viv on her way out the door that day, and when the screen door had already shut I said, We'll see. We'll see, I said again to myself as I went out to the porch, watched Viv disappear down the street, and then I sat down in the rocking chair and thought, Why not? rocking, and imagining what my life would be like if I stayed another week, another month even, years. In the late afternoons I'd go to the bar, before it filled with the dense musk of men, and watch Viv and Kim as they worked. I'd slowly sip my one whiskey soda that was actually three. Later I'd sit on Viv's porch and wait for her to come home. When she did we would rock in our rocking chairs and watch the sky change colors. Both of us would be drunk, or one of us drunk and the other dead, until we switched places again. The rhythm of our rocking would be slightly out of sync. At some point I'd go up to bed, though I wouldn't be able to sleep, and even if I did nod off for a moment I'd wake again with a start, because branches in the forest behind the house would be snapping or preparing to snap.

X.

There was a fight that night at the bar. I was sitting in the corner watching Viv and Kim when from the back room came a sharp crack. At the same moment the man next to me grabbed the throat of the man next to him, shoved him to the floor, straddled his hips, and started pummeling him fist over fist. I watched in the circle of watching eyes, we all watched as if hypnotized into a collective stillness by that sudden snarling of flesh.

When Viv stepped up on the porch much later I asked her if she was alright. Rather than answering me immediately she sat down and slowly rolled herself a cigarette. Then she exhaled a lungful of smoke and said, That kind of thing happens all the time. Comes with the territory I guess. I seemed to hear those sentences twice, as if they had echoed inside my mind, and I kept hearing them again for the rest of the night, when I'd gone to bed but couldn't fall asleep, my nerves still twitching with heat. When dawn came I heard her rocking in her chair, as if she'd stayed there all through the night, and I imagined her many years later, her skin dried out by the wind, her face turned to ash, still rocking on her rotten porch.

XI.

In the morning I got in my car. Instead of heading immediately for the border I drove in the opposite direction, going north along that relentless road. Direction didn't seem to matter on a road that never varied, that only stretched its monotony to infinity, though for the moment at least I knew exactly where I was going. I remembered the turn-off and the gravel road that wound its way towards the coast. I stepped carefully over the rotten boards, then climbed the stairs to the attic room and stood staring out at the sea. One of us had never left. One of us was already a ghost. I turned around, targeted the eye of a camera targeting me, and walked towards it.

DISMEMBERMENT PLAN

I'm thinking about god tonight. I don't know why. I don't like the idea of god. I don't like thinking about the idea of god. When I think of god, I imagine someone tinkering with my emotions in cruel, unpredictable ways. It's like god has one of those soundboards that music producers use, with all the knobs and dials and blinking lights, and he sits up there in his sound-proof room fiddling around with the levels. God doesn't care what we make, or do, or even what we think; he only cares how we feel. He slouches in his chair like some kind of hulking, middle-aged metal head, with greasy hair and bad teeth, and he mumbles to himself, saying things like, Big fear tonight, massive overwhelming fear, heavy, inescapable feeling of dread. And then he cranks up the levels.

I look at my clock. It's just after six. I've been lying on my bed for a couple hours, doing nothing, just thinking, and now, when I try to get up, there's a weight on my chest that feels like one of those lead blankets dentists use when they x-ray your teeth. I look around, sensing that some kind of invisible film, infinitely thin, has slid itself in between me and my room, so that my own things, the few objects I can actually call mine, now seem completely indifferent to me, even alien to me—

We're going to have to cut our way out.

We're going to have to cut our way out is the sentence that pops into my head, from a movie I've seen, I can't remember the title, in which a group of space explorers discovers that the entire planet they've landed on is one giant, desperately hungry organism, and realizing this a bit too late one of them says, in a grim, determined tone, *We're going to have to cut our way out*, the sentence now on repeat in my head as I get up and go downstairs, to the living room, where my dad is sitting on the couch, his feet up on the coffee table, watching TV. Or not watching TV, it's more like the TV is watching him, because he's asleep, his mouth is open, he's snoring slightly, and he's only wearing one sock. His bare foot looks pale, livid, like something that should be in a jar, preserved in formaldehyde, like one of those fetal pigs I had to dissect in biology class, pickled, wrinkly, and so white it's impossible not to look at, it's completely dominating the room, and dominating my dad, like it's hypnotized him. I notice that even the weatherman, who's calling for isolated showers, can't avoid addressing the foot, he's giving his forecast to the foot, the whole world has been reduced to just him and the foot.

    I go into the kitchen. I find a note my mom has left on the counter, saying she'll be home late, I should get leftovers from the fridge, so I open the door and am immediately confronted by an enormous number of jars, things floating eerily inside of jars, olives, pickles, hard-boiled eggs, maraschino cherries, artichoke hearts, something that looks like shriveled ears—I'm still under the influence of the foot, I can't shake the foot, I half expect to find, at the back of this mausoleum of jars, my dad's foot, floating, in a jar, in formaldehyde—

    I shut the door. I sit down at the table. I can hear the news coming from the TV: a polar bear, born in captivity at the local zoo, has just been released, on an experimental trial, into the wilderness of the Arctic—when my sister comes in, wearing a hoodie and jeans, her hair pulled back in a ponytail. She goes straight to the fridge and opens it, pulls out the lasagna, dishes herself a piece, puts it in the microwave, then pours herself a glass of orange juice, all seemingly in a single motion, as if she knew, in advance, exactly what she was going to do, had drawn up the action in her head, then executed it, without the slightest hesitation, perfectly smoothly, as if her whole reality were made of some kind of creamy, hypoallergenic substance, a fancy brand of hand lotion maybe—and then she sits down next to me and says, "What's up?"

"Nothing."

"Mom tell you where she is?"

"Nope."

Now she's retrieving her lasagna from the microwave, grabbing a fork from the drawer, sitting down again, and digging in. She's eating fast. She's already moving *past* the lasagna, already digesting that solid mass of meat and cheese as if it were nothing. Now she's walking towards the sink, rinsing her dish in the sink, then putting it in the dishwasher. She has a way of almost *bouncing* as she moves, as if a system of pneumatic pumps pulsed inside her, so that the whole kitchen, in fact, starts bouncing up and down; she seems to have brought space into a kind of rhythmic accord with her own being, I'm already anticipating the moment when the blender bursts into song, then the microwave, then the refrigerator and the dishwasher; reality itself will soon have transformed into some hideously cheesy musical in homage to my sister and her gleeful, radiant personality—I want to grab a knife from the drawer, go into the living room, cut dad's foot off, bring the severed bleeding thing back into the kitchen and hold it up in front of her, shaking it, shouting *look at this, look at it*—but then she goes upstairs, she's suddenly gone, and I'm just sitting there, alone, in the kitchen, staring at my hands.

A blank spot, a void. I seem to cease experiencing reality for a while. Then I'm startled back into consciousness by the sound of the TV shutting off. It's dad. He's awake. He's rubbing his face, I bet, as he moves towards me, and I can sense the whole space-time continuum of the kitchen adjust to his now mobile form, almost like he's a massive, ambulant space-time suck pit, inhaling reality and breathing it out. I hear him—no, I *feel* him breathing, the air around me contracting, growing more dense and moist—and then his hand, like a condensation of that dense and moist dad air, comes to rest on my shoulder. I can see his reflection in the kitchen window, and my own reflection too: there we are, father and son, reflected. He's staring at me through the reflection, he's in front of me and behind me at the same time, just hovering there, as if this weren't a completely psychotic thing to do, as if it weren't going to be burned traumatically into my brain for the rest of my life—

"Find something to eat?" he says, and begins sort of rubbing-patting my shoulder—it's not a back rub, but it's not a simple pat on the shoulder either—it's a hybrid kind of rub-pat, which doesn't even exist, as far as I know—

"Yeah."

"Good," he says, and then gives my shoulder a little squeeze, definitely a squeeze, as he adds, "Put some meat on those bones," the word "meat" corresponding exactly to the moment of the squeeze, so that it's a meat-squeeze, or maybe a squeeze-meat. I start to wonder in what kind of world, what kind of reality, is it okay for a dad to say "put some meat on those bones" to his son, especially when, just minutes ago, it seemed plausible, even likely, that his foot would be found in the refrigerator, pickled, in a jar—essentially my dad is demanding that I put some of *his* meat on *my* bones, so that I too can one day become the kind of man he is: I'll ghost through the house, my mouth open, breathing loudly, half-asleep, half-alive, terrorizing the helpless members of my family—

"Well," he says, breathing in through his nose, "it's dark already, isn't it," and then he squeezes my shoulder one more time, and drifts out of the kitchen, leaving that strange, oblique sentence behind him, like some sinister prophecy of the present. It's dark already. No shit, dad. I grab my jacket, check my back pocket for my wallet, and slip out through the back door, into the alley.

The alley is dark, already, and crowded with vegetation, with ivy covering a fence, with overgrown bushes or trees from the neighbors' houses, and there's a rich, dank, vegetal smell to everything, which I find myself inhaling hungrily—I need more oxygen, I decide, more plant matter—*nature*, it suddenly occurs to me, is the key, it's the solution to everything; and as I come to the end of the alley and cross the street, I'm thinking maybe I'll drop out of school, head for the woods, immerse myself in wilderness, climb some mountains, try to grow a beard—and I'm at the part with the beard when I push through the door to the mini-mart, buy a bagel with cream cheese, sit down at one of the little plastic tables, and start trying to solve the complex problem of the saran wrap, which encases the bagel in an impenetrable shroud. I tear and pick and pull and pry; I start using my teeth; I feel myself losing control, like a starved animal I am now maniacally gnawing at the plastic—for a second I have the appalling sensation that I'm somehow trapped *inside* the saran wrap, that it's engulfing me, suffocating me—I get up and go to the counter, grab a plastic knife, return to my table, and, with a visceral, almost savage feeling of relief, stab the knife straight through the center of the bagel and breathe, breathe—for some reason I haven't been breathing.

I eat. The bagel is dry, the cream cheese sticks to the top of my mouth. I wonder if I might spontaneously forget how to accomplish my body's most basic functions and die, just suddenly die, from sheer stupidity. I'm not prepared for this thought, I don't know what to do with it; ideas are deadly, I decide, because nature doesn't know how to handle them, they're these anomalous burps in the order of life, these random ejaculations of nonbeing, these holes, which reality can fall into at any second. I scrunch the saran wrap into a little ball and begin batting it back and forth across the table, using my hands as paddles, increasing the speed, flicking my wrists, right wrist left wrist, faster and faster, until a woman comes into the mini-mart, maybe in her forties, very professional, in a skirt and jacket, high heels, a handbag tucked under her arm. She asks for a bottle of whiskey from the guy, puts a twenty down on the counter, gets her change, slides the bottle into her handbag, and leaves. I watch her walk through the parking lot, she doesn't get into a car, but strides away down the street, maybe towards the park, where she'll sit on a bench, under the moon, with her bottle of whiskey, alone—I'm through the door, through the parking lot, and on the street about fifty feet behind her, a crackling and hissing inside my brain—my brain actually feels like one of those electric mosquito killers people hang on their porches, with images zooming in, I'm sitting next to her on the bench and then zap! she's handing me the bottle and then zap! her warm whiskey breath and then zap! my charred corpse collapsed on the ground, I slow down, I'm relieved, actually relieved, when she walks up a driveway, opens a door, and goes into a house.

    I turn around, start walking home. I should be tagged, I decide, so that cops and psychologists can track me down with radio signals. The houses seem to know this too, they're hiding behind their carefully-trimmed hedges, protecting themselves with white, thick-framed windows, isolated, sealed, quarantined, vacuum-packed. They press together, grow taller and more austere, monolithic, like refrigerators, especially the new ones with sleek, streamlined facades, their expressionless faces probably hiding an enormous number of jars, jars of pickled feet, pickled noses and ears, pickled fingers and toes, the skin of them pruned, white, translucent—

I start to wonder if maybe all houses eventually wind up destroying us. In my mind for some reason I'm explaining this idea in history class, I'm suggesting that even our most impressive buildings, our mansions, our skyscrapers, will eventually come down and crush us, that at some point they'll turn our brains into pulp, and I'm waiting for this kid Brian, with the shaggy hair, who always disagrees with me, who attacks me for no reason at all, to say something stupid, like, But what about the Parthenon? at which point I'll ask him if he has any experience of what it's like to actually *live* in the Parthenon, because what I'm talking about isn't being *physically* crushed by the things we build, though that happens too—I'm talking about being *psychologically* mangled, broken down, mashed up, pulverized; and I'd like Brian to provide a single example, just a single example of a structure that does not, over time, spiritually crush anyone who inhabits it, just one example of a human construction that does not suffocate and eventually destroy every one of its occupants—and since Brian just sits there stupidly with his mouth open, unable to come up with even a single example, I rest my case, I walk on, victoriously, towards the park, where hundreds, possibly thousands of frogs are croaking, in unison, like applause—

But then they stop. Right when I enter the park, they suddenly stop. All at once they go silent, and a thick hush spreads over the pond. I sit down on a bench. I pick up some pebbles from the ground, begin tossing them into the pond, glumly at first, even bitterly—but soon I become entirely entranced by the satisfying sound each pebble makes as it plunks into the pond, so clear, so crisp and round; I'm discovering that by managing the timing of my tosses just right, I can stifle the thoughts that try to enter my head, I can drown them, sink them—*plunk plunk plunk*: the day's humiliations, failures, agitations, all gone, all drowned, all gone down to the bottom of the pond. I even start taunting them, my enemies, daring them to come up again, just try, you fuckers, to rise up again—I sit there waiting for the next assault, a pebble at the ready, cocked back in my hand, an arsenal of pebbles in the other; and when nothing comes, when I sense not even the slightest inkling of an agitation or the merest stirring in the murk, I lean back, I lace my fingers behind my head, and feel, for a moment, perfectly calm.

It's inevitable that at the exact moment I discover this deep and potentially abiding sense of peace, a man walks by with one of those small, snorting, smashed-faced dogs, the ones that can't really breathe, that have been specifically designed to be unable to breathe, to choke on themselves, to suffocate inside their own facial anatomy, and of course this dog has to stop by my bench and take a crap, and I'm supposed to just sit there watching it crap, because we've decided this is fine, to let one's dog take a shit directly in front of a person trying to enjoy a moment of peace—this is okay, we've said collectively, especially when the man bends down, responsible dog owner that he is, and picks up the shit in a bag, and now swings it happily as he walks away, as if it's a wonderful thing, a truly wonderful thing, to swing a bag of shit in one's hand—

I walk home. That little bit of quietude is gone, blown up by the dog, the shit-bag dog with its suffocation face, unsinkable by any pebble. I turn down the alley. I start sucking in the air with greedy inhalations, trying to get that sensation again, nature, my life in the woods, roots, berries, rocks. Nothing. I go in through the back door. There's no one in the kitchen, no one in the living room, but the lights are still on, the TV is still on, as if the house is pursuing a life of its own even in the absence of its occupants, it doesn't seem to care that no one is here, it has its own rhythms and cycles, the refrigerator is humming along, the dishwasher is churning and chortling, hot air pumps through the heating ducts—I turn off the lights in the kitchen, go into the living room to kill the TV, and there, on the floor, at the base of the coffee table, is my dad's sock, like a pile of skin left behind on a plate.

WHAT WAS LEFT

Most days, after school, I go out to the forest behind my house. It's filled with all kinds of things: old washing machines, refrigerators, toilets and sinks, water heaters, ironing boards, microwaves. They're all wedged into the ground at odd angles, like someone threw them out the window of a house. But there's no house, just bushes and brambles and trees.

There's an aquarium I found that's filled up with rainwater, with three brown salamanders living in it. I think of those salamanders as mine. Their bodies have a kind of light in them, a strange orange light that comes from inside. They hardly move, though I'm sure they could crawl out of the aquarium if they wanted.

When it starts to get dark, I walk back to my house. Coming from the woods, the house always looks a little gloomy, like some dark wing has spread itself over the roof.

—

My mother is usually asleep on the couch. She sleeps on the couch a lot these days, her body in the shape of a bean. Every once in a while, her eyes open and she mumbles, I'll be back in just a minute. Then she falls asleep again.

She used to be the opposite. When I was still in middle school she was on the move all the time. She'd pick me up from school and drive me to the mall and start grabbing things off the racks. She loved to see me dressed in new clothes. We'd come out of those stores carrying hundreds of bags and then we'd go to a restaurant. She couldn't stop telling me how perfect I was. Isn't he perfect? she'd say to the waiters.

One night she spoke in a hushed voice. She leaned across the table and said she had something to tell me. I could feel the heat coming off her face. She took my left hand, and pointed to the scar on one side. When you were born, she said, you had a little finger here, an extra one. The doctors said we had to remove it, because it would cause problems. So they did an operation, and afterwards everything was fine. But I kept the finger, Oliver. It was too special to lose. I couldn't let them throw away a part of you, not a single part. I kept it in a special little box. Someday, when you're older, I'll give it to you, but until then no one can know. It's your special secret, yours and mine, okay?

My mother never mentioned the finger again. I've searched the whole house while she's asleep, but I've never found the little box. Maybe my father took it with him when he left. Maybe he threw it away.

———

In my English class, we're reading fairy tales. For homework we had to write one ourselves. I went home and wrote:

> Once upon a time, there was a village where people were losing their eyes. The birds in the region were plucking them out. No one knew why. People would reach for the places where their eyes used to be, and find nothing. At the edge of the village, near the forest, lived a little girl. The birds would come to her window at night, and drop the villagers' eyes into jars the girl

held out to them. She stored the jars in her closet. She kept them all to herself.

When Ms. Jacobs read my story, she asked me to stay after class.

"This is a very intriguing story, Oliver," she said.

I didn't say anything. I assumed something bad was about to happen.

"Do you mind if I ask why the girl is keeping the villagers' eyes in her closet?"

"She's friends with the birds," I said.

"Ah," said Ms. Jacobs. "And what does she plan to do with them?"

"I don't know."

Ms. Jacobs laughed. Her eyes flashed when she laughed. Then she leaned forward. "That's not how a story works, Oliver. You need to keep writing. This isn't finished."

But I don't know how to finish my story. I don't even know what it means. Why did Ms. Jacobs laugh, and what did I see when her eyes flashed? A little opening. A long dark lane through a tunnel of trees. Something.

—

I broke my mother's promise today. It was during one of our drills. We were huddled under our desks, waiting for someone to come, and I was scratching my scar. It gets itchy sometimes, and the skin around it turns red. Iris noticed and passed me a note. *I have one of those too*, said her note. I flipped the note over and wrote, *Meet me in the woods after school*.

We met in the woods. She showed me her scar, which is almost the exact same as mine. I told her the story my mother told me. She thought the part about the special box was gross. If I were you, she said, I'd find that thing and throw it away. What did they do with yours? I said. I don't know, she said. Burned it I guess. You know, in those incinerators they have in hospitals.

We walked down to the bunkers. Iris knows her way around the bunkers much better than me. She led me back into the darker rooms, which had mattresses in them, even bookshelves. She said her ex-boyfriend used to take her there all the time. He was totally obsessed with this place, she said. He thought people lived here during the war. He had this theory that they were the only ones who survived, and that everyone else is actually dead. We're all a bunch of zombies according to him. He was a total weirdo though.

Later, when we were walking back to our houses, I asked Iris if she ever felt strange. I meant because of her scar. You know, like you're an alien or something. She stopped walking. She looked at me. You're not going to get all obsessed with this, are you? she said. Then she kept walking.

—

Tonight I had a strange discussion with my mother. She wasn't fully awake, but her eyes were open at least some of the time. She said she didn't want me to think that my father left because of me. You can never think it was your fault, Oliver, she said. She reached out to squeeze my hand. Then she closed her eyes again. Some people, she said, have motors in them that never turn off. Your father is one of those people.

I remember the night my father left. He woke me up in the middle of the night and told me he was going on a journey. He said he'd lost something extremely important and had to go on the journey to find it. He said that in life people had different cars, and that he'd heard about a boat trip to the Arctic. He wasn't sure when he'd return, but he knew someday we'd meet again.

Before he left, he was working on a car parked in our driveway. I'd come home from school and find him with his head under the hood, like the car had eaten the upper half of him. He kept taking out parts and replacing them with new ones. The car would cough and grumble and moan, but he couldn't get it to start. He'd come into the house all grumpy and covered in grease.

But at dinner sometimes my father would get excited. He'd tell us that soon, when the car was running, we'd go on a trip as a family. He had this idea that one day we'd drive across the border. Up there, he said, there was never any war, and the trees are bigger than anything you've ever seen. I've heard they don't have a government. You know what that means, Ollie? No speed limits!

The car is still parked in the driveway. Some parts of the engine sit on the back seat, and one of the front tires is flat. My mother keeps saying she's going to have it towed, but then doesn't.

—

Last night I went to my first fire. Iris was the one who knew where it was, in the parking lot behind the old mill. I think she liked the idea that she was taking me to my first one. Her face had a kind of sheen on it. You're going to love this, she said, leaning into me.

The fire was already big by the time we got there. People were burning old clothes and furniture from their parents' houses, and books from school, and cardboard boxes full of all kinds of things. Some of the things wouldn't burn. They just sat there surrounded by the flames, like holes you could almost put your hand through. Iris pulled me close to the fire and took an envelope from inside her jacket. What is it? I said. She said it was just some crazy shit her ex-boyfriend had written. She threw it on the flames and watched it burn and then asked me what I'd brought. I couldn't think of anything to bring, I said. Loser, she said, and laughed. Then she pulled me over to a group of people she knew. They were drinking, and Iris took the bottle, drank, and passed it to me. The liquor burned through the wall between the fire and me and I remember laughing, screaming, and leaping up like a lick of the flames. Later I was sitting on a tire, staring at the shape of the steel mill, trying to remember why I'd screamed. Iris had fallen asleep.

—

I've started sitting in my father's car after school. I sit in the driver's seat, prop my notebook on the steering wheel, and try to think about my story. But usually I wind up just thinking about Ms. Jacobs. I keep going back to the moment when she laughed, when her eyes flashed, and I saw that lane stretching through the tunnel of trees. Sometimes I think I can hear her whispering in my ear. *Your story still isn't finished, Oliver.*

Eventually I fall asleep, and the parts of my story turn in my dreams. They're all in the wrong places. The people in the village have beaks. The girl's glass jar is full of stones. The father comes home with the girl's eyes stuffed in his pockets. She has talons instead of toes. And the birds are just masses of bloody feathers perched on the gutters of the house. They aren't really even birds.

Later I go back into the house. I make some macaroni for my mother and me, turn on the television and watch the news. There's a story about a storm somewhere else, and a story about a lost dog, and a story about vacations to the moon. I eat macaroni at the kitchen table. Every once in a while, my mother wakes up and says, I'll be back in just a minute. Then she falls asleep again.

I take the extra chair from the kitchen table out with me into the woods, set it down by the aquarium, and sit there for a long time. Eventually the moon moves into a gap between the trees, and lights up the washing machines, the microwaves, the bathtubs and sinks. I watch my salamanders drift towards the bottom of the tank. Somehow they stop before they touch down, and just hang there, hovering, suspended. Their fingers are spread, their black eyes gleam, and a soft glow is coming from their throats.

BLACK BOX

I

Daniel's mother was the mother I wanted, my real mother, my true mother, my friend. My parents had voted for Reagan that year and I'd pledged never to set foot in their house again, so I was always riding the bus around town, my backpack stuffed full of books and tapes and a toothbrush, my brain crazy with too much caffeine. I stayed with Inez and Maeve, I stayed anywhere I could, but I was always coming back to Daniel's, even when Daniel wasn't there. His mother had a job I wanted, at a theater downtown, and records I wanted, and books I wanted, and long silver hair I wanted and a way of dressing I wanted and years full of travel to places I wanted to have traveled to. I wanted her memories. I wanted her brain. I couldn't understand how Daniel could be such a mess, so flustered by his weather of fears, when he had a mother like his, who let us do all the things our mothers would never let us do. On weekends she would give us wine, she thought it was fine if we had a little wine at her house, just a glass or two, so we wouldn't go out and get drunk at the Pier. Of course we also got drunk at the Pier, but those nights at Daniel's were just as important, maybe even more important for me, especially when her friends came over, artists and people from the theater, and she'd drift around, chatting and refilling our glasses. She had a way of resting her hand on my shoulder, just for a moment or two, not pressing, just resting it there like some calm, quiet, companionable animal presence.

One day she gave me the key. We were in her kitchen, drinking earl grey tea, and I'd said something about how frustrating it was, that my parents wanted me to get good grades and go to college when they'd also just voted for my annihilation, for everyone's annihilation, for the annihilation of the whole world, and she looked at me over the rim of her mug, the steam wafting over her face, misting her eyes, her steel blue eyes. Here, she said, then opened a drawer, pulled out a key with a leather tag on the ring, and pressed it into my hand, her two warm hands cupping mine now holding the key.

I kept that key in a special inner pocket of my backpack. I became a little obsessed with it, checking that pocket all the time. When I had to go home for more clothes, I'd take out the key on the bus, turn it around in my hands, rub the worn leather tag. Her name had been pressed into the leather: Monique Tremblay. And as I walked up the hill, insects zooming through the orange glow of the streetlights, night birds singing in the trees, I whispered that name to myself, as if the person walking home wasn't me. I looked up at a planet hovering like a slow-burning eye on the horizon, and wondered if there were stars that traveled without the organizing circles of orbits, that just drifted around, untethered to anything, in perpetual, patternless flight. At the bottom of the driveway I paused, staring up at the stark grey shape of my house, with its backdrop of gangly trees. For some reason the light in my bedroom was on. The thought that bled through my porous brain was that my own face would appear in that window, that I'd find myself staring at me.

—

When summer came, I got a job working the register at a bakery on Capitol Hill. It was my first ever job, and I was so happy to be making money that I messed up everyone's orders, served people muffins when they asked for scones, gave them back way too much change. My brain was always fast-forwarding into the future, to the moment when I'd get my first paycheck, when I'd buy a car, and find a place to live on my own, and go on road trips to California and Alaska, and buy more clothes, whole closets full of outrageous outfits, so I'd never have to go back home to do my laundry. I'd skip college and work at Monique's theater, where I'd design costumes and sets, or run the lights and the sound, or buy coffee and cigarettes for the actors. Once she'd let me into rehearsals, and I'd sat cocooned in the empty theater, watching the actors doing their warm-ups, contorting their faces and mouths, making animal sounds, passing invisible objects between one another. They looked like people who had just been born and didn't yet know how their bodies worked. Once the rehearsal started they stiffened, the magic of the moment was gone, so in the theater company I'd start in the future there would only be warm-ups, improvisations, plays that weren't really plays, with sets like dreams or collages. I imagined all this while working the register, giving people tens when they'd paid with fives, until the bakers in the back started cracking jokes about my math.

There was one named Jake who joined me on my breaks, when I sat on a milk crate reading novels. The rings on his fingers made me think he belonged to some secret society of sorcerers or assassins or thieves. He didn't say much, just smoked and asked what I was reading, and looked at me with one eye, like a whale that only lifts one eye from the sea. One day we happened to be leaving the bakery at the same time, and wound up walking through the park together, and I asked him about his rings, if they meant something. He said he thought of the rings as dials, and then he clasped a ring between his thumb and his middle finger, and turned it a little, and said it was sort of like turning down the volume. His fingers were skinny and long, his knuckles like knots. I asked him if he could also turn the volume up, and he paused, and said it was a good question, but that he didn't know because he'd never tried. Mostly I need to turn it down, he said, and chuckled sort of grimly.

We started going to movies. We'd see whatever was playing at the Varsity or the Egyptian or the Harvard Exit, art films or horror films or documentaries, though if there was a horror film playing I'd usually insist that we see it. I loved watching people make terrible decisions. I loved the moment when they walked into the house they never should have walked into, opened the door they never should have opened, kept going when they should have turned around. Sometimes people in the audience would whisper, *Don't do it, don't do it*, and someone else would whisper, *Do it, do it*, and I started doing this too, talking to the characters, warning them or egging them on, while Jake sat with his hands attached to the armrests. Afterwards we'd walk around, talking about the parts we liked or didn't like. Eventually I learned that Jake didn't like horror movies at all, he kept his eyes closed through most of them. Why didn't you tell me? I said, and he shrugged and twisted his rings and said he'd thought it might be better watching them with me. But it wasn't? I said, and he said, Nope, and we laughed and then changed the topic.

One night he told me he was moving to Alaska. We'd just had sex for the first time, and it hadn't been quite as scary and awful and traumatizing as the other two times I'd had sex, which gave me the idea that sex might actually be enjoyable at some distant point in the future, if Reagan hadn't already vaporized everything by then. Afterwards we'd gone to see a film, which was so laughably bad that we'd loved it and couldn't stop talking about it, couldn't stop cracking up at the incredible terribleness of it, our stomachs cramping we were laughing so hard, until we got to the University Bridge, when Jake started twisting his rings. He was always twisting them but that night there was something different about it, the way he went from thumb to pinky and back again, turning each ring twice, machine-like and sort of maniacal, like some assembly line system that couldn't stop. And then he said he was moving to Alaska, and he kind of elongated the word, made a shape with it, something huge, like a ship going under the bridge. He looked at me with his eye, his whale eye, which by now had migrated all the way to one side of his face. I said, That's great, because what else was I supposed to say, we'd just had sex for the first time and we'd talked about Alaska a lot, the jobs you could get in Alaska, the money you could make, and he said, Yeah, I'm pretty excited, and I said, That's really great, and felt like someone had punched me in the stomach.

—

When it finally arrived, my first paycheck, for three hundred and forty-two dollars, I started looking for rooms. I poured over want ads in the weekly, made calls from the bakery and set up meetings and took the bus to neighborhoods I'd never been to, and I toured houses inhabited by cat ladies and horticulturists, massage therapists, booksellers, strippers, social workers, psychics, record store owners, antiquarians. Some of the houses were so cluttered I could hardly squeeze through the halls. The relentless rain had soaked through their walls and made blots of mold on the baseboards. Some people said I didn't have enough money. A few said I was too young. Finally I found an old gay man on Aloha Street. He wasn't actually that old, his white-bearded face beamed with a kind of boyishness, wrinkles grinned in the corners of his eyes. He didn't care that I couldn't pay the deposit. Deposits are for paranoid people, he said cheerfully as he led me into his living room, which was full of plants, buddhas, and penises. Opera was blasting from the speakers. A small yellow bird flitted around in a cage. That's Evelyn, he said. His name was Paul. The room he was renting was simple and small, just a bed and a desk, with a photograph of a man hanging on the wall. I can't really say I moved in, since I didn't have much to move in with, just the same backpack I lugged around everywhere. But I took out my toothbrush and put it in the bathroom, and stacked my books and tapes on the desk, and slipped off my shoes and danced around, as the opera coming from the living room made everything grand and dramatic.

    I loved my life in that room. There was one little window that looked out on the backyard, where an old maple tree stood, and when I got home in the late afternoon the sun would be filtering through the bright green leaves, making patterns like Japanese screens, and I'd open the window and let the breezes come in, and sit on my bed reading novels or drawing in my sketchbook. Sometimes Paul would come in and set a glass of iced tea on my desk, and then slip out, his entrances and exits timed to the moments of the opera in which he starred. On the night when I decided to chop off my hair, he came home, wearing his black leather jacket and chaps, and offered to touch up the back. He'd been a barber a long time ago, he said, in one of the many lives he had lived—and as he draped a towel over my shoulders and started to snip, he told me about his life as a bartender and a landscape architect, a tour guide, a construction worker, a teacher, a chef, a taxi driver and an acupuncturist. Now he worked as a nurse in a hospice. So you see a lot of people die? I said, and he sighed and said, I try.

That night, when I finally got into bed, I lay awake for a long time, with the lights out, listening to the stirring of the maple leaves. They stirred even when there was no wind, like children dangling their legs off the end of a dock. The moon rose behind the house and lit up the photo of the man on the wall. His face filled most of the frame, and he was leaning towards the camera, smiling, while behind him, slightly blurry, was the bow of the boat he was rowing. He was leaning forward to pull on the oars, and the person taking the photo was sitting in the stern. The shot was overexposed, so the water was almost white, silver-white waves blurring into the sky. Suddenly I knew, without knowing how, that the man in the photo was dead, that he used to live in this room, and that Paul had taken the photo from the back of the boat. The dead man was rowing on the silver-white waves, and I was living in his room, sleeping in the bed where he'd slept, while outside, in the night full of doves, the maple leaves stirred without wind.

—

Since the beginning of summer Daniel had been talking about his father a lot, rerouting every conversation back to his father, returning incessantly to the subject of his father, who was a filmmaker and lived in Montreal, where Daniel said he wanted to move, after high school he'd move to Montreal and work with his father on films, there was a documentary he was making about people who abandoned their lives, changed their jobs and sometimes even their names, and claimed no memory of the people they'd formerly been. Daniel had always been interested in these kinds of things, lucid dreams, near-death experiences, hypnosis, mysticism, psychedelic drugs, but there was something a little suspicious about his way of talking about his father and the film, the suddenness of it, he'd hardly mentioned his father before and now he was indifferent to everything else—when he couldn't steer conversation back to his father, he'd sink into a thick, impenetrable gloom, a dark swamp of irritability and sullenness, his shoulders curled inward with contempt. Around Monique he became unreachable and rude. He answered her questions with monosyllables, short dull blasts of boredom and abuse. One day he came home with a video camera and started filming her, we were sitting around simply talking when he aimed the lens at her face. You're on film, he said, in a voice unlike his own voice, more granular and aggressive, as if a stranger had broken into the house. When Monique asked him to put the thing down he refused. I'm gathering evidence, he said, and zoomed in on her.

    I stopped coming around, or only coming when I knew he wouldn't be there. We'd been good friends for a while, in our first year of high school, when Inez and Daniel and Maeve and I had been almost inseparable, but he was beginning to frighten me now, the way he lurched around the house, veering unpredictably from room to room, appearing suddenly with his camera. I still saw him every once in a while at the Pier, where he'd begun showing up with a new friend, someone I'd never seen before, tall, gaunt, with sloping shoulders and the eerie blue glow of glaciers in his eyes. The moment I saw him the thought arrived unbidden in my brain that he wasn't entirely real, that Daniel had somehow projected him.

—

After work some days I'd walk down to Pioneer Square, dodging the scattered heaps of homeless people, and push through the door of the old brick building on First, and climb the creaking stairs to the second floor, where Monique's theater was the third door down on the right. I'd sneak into the back row, doing my best to be invisible, slumping down, pulling my knees up to my chest. I loved watching Monique work with her actors, the way she moved around them, talked to them, and touched them, as if she were wrapping them in some magical fabric, some invisible scrim that made them transparent to themselves, like those deep sea fish whose organs were visible underneath their translucent skin. The play they were making was about a silent woman whose silence drives everyone insane. She was played by a woman named Anne, who was sharp and wiry and small, with short dark hair and bright green eyes that startled from her chiseled skull. I envied her, the way she worked with Monique, privately and quietly and close, the two of them sitting cross-legged on the stage, their faces in profile like a puzzle. Sometimes their lips didn't move, as if they were communicating at a deeper level than language or even than thought. Monique had asked her to study Butoh, she wanted her movement in the play to be a continual dance, stunned, slow, and completely at odds with everything that was happening around her. The other characters were courting her and plotting to kill her, but she moved through their frenzy like an animal attuned to other things. The moment she slipped into her role I was rapt. I felt her face in my face. I felt her eyes in my eyes. Her whole body moved inside of mine.

After rehearsal I'd walk home, enveloped by the cool light of dusk. At that hour, a trace of the theater seemed to slip outside and touch the faces of people in the street, exaggerating their gestures and glances, sharpening their cheekbones and chins.

I'd weave through the crowds in the slow stunned way of the silent woman, both detached from things and somehow alert to them. Later, when I got home, I'd lie on my bed for a long time, listening to the sound of the maple leaves. I wondered if people could be born more than once. I wondered if the light in my other room was still on. I pulled the sheets up to my chin, held them there in my fists, blinked and then blinked again.

—

And then one day I got lost in the halls behind the theater. I'd been in the dressing room with Monique, talking about silence, the thickness of the silent woman's silence, how thick she wanted it to be, how impenetrable, and when she left I'd gone out the backstage door, looking for a bathroom, and found myself in a long hall lined with identical doors and lit with dim skittish lights. I started trying doors, all of them locked, and took a left at the end of the hall, then a right, wondering how I'd never discovered this part of the theater before. Finally a door opened into a bare room with painted wooden floors and a desk where a man leaned back in his chair watching television and talking on the phone. He hung up when I came in, looked me up and down and said, You here for an audition? and I said no, I was looking for a bathroom, and he paused, pushed his bottom lip out, and looked me up and down again, more slowly this time, more deliberate, his thumb stroking the underside of his chin. You sure? he said, and I said yes, I was sure I was looking for a bathroom, and he held his eyes on me for one more second, then shrugged, returned his gaze to the television, and said, Two doors down on your left.

I left that room, I walked out quickly and closed the door behind me, but later, when school had started, I'd be sitting in class, the voice of my teacher droning on like some radio station from another era, and the word *audition* would pop into my head, and suddenly I'd be in that room again, under the gaze of that man again, feeling the viscosity of his eyes, the thickness and heaviness of his eyelids, the dead star density of his exhaustion.

—

I went to see my parents once a month. That was our agreement. My father would pick me up at the bus stop in his huge, hyperventilating car, the radio blaring about the prospect of market collapse, and we'd drive up the hill to the house. My mother would be talking on the phone, in the voice she used to talk on the phone, high-pitched and saccharine, like a carnival ride of candied clichés. It made me almost sick to my stomach to hear the sound of that jubilant voice, so happy to stockpile hydrogen bombs and deny the existence of AIDS. Over dinner I told a lot of lies, about how much money I was saving, how Monique had promised to pay me for the next play, how we were going to take the company on tour to Europe and the UK. I piled lie upon lie, stacking them up like paper plates, until my parents tried to change the topic. Then I'd excuse myself, put my dishes in the dishwasher, and climb the stairs to my room.

I hated that room, felt haunted by it, inhabited by it, but still, every time I went to my parents' house, I was summoned, at some point, up the stairs, down the long hall, to the dark door at the end. The line of light under that door was like the mute mouth of a scream. I'd slip inside, taking care to step softly for some reason, as if I might startle some sleeping presence to life. I'd check the boxes in the closet and the bottom drawers in the dresser, making sure all the things I'd left behind hadn't bred, that they hadn't spawned some terrible clone from my skin cells, strands of my hair, the slimy residue of my recurring bad dreams.

I'd turn off the light and shut the door behind me, then go back downstairs, where my mother would be waiting to drive me home. She wouldn't let me take the bus. She loved holding me captive in her car so that she could needle me with questions. Was I seeing anyone, was I happy, was I considering taking ballet class perhaps, was I practicing for the SAT? But then, as we approached my house, she began making breathing noises through her nose, quick inhalations, especially when she saw a black person walking down the street. You know, she said when she stopped in front of my house, you can always come home.

—

One day near the end of summer my manager at work handed me an envelope. I took it out back and sat on my milk crate and opened it. It was a letter from Jake:

Dear Esther,

I guess it sort of occurred to me after I got here that maybe the timing of my departure wasn't so great. I don't want to presume anything but I just thought I should explain that for me there was suddenly this feeling that something between us might get big and borderless and uncontainable and that I'd have to find ways to contain it and that my ways of containing it might not be so good for either of us. So I went to Alaska. On the plane I stared out the window and thought the landscape looked like wrinkled sheets. Some specks down there might have been migrating elk. That's all. I hope you're well. I'll be back in Seattle in September.

-Jake

I read the letter twice, then went back to the register. It was busy that afternoon, and as I served the customers and accepted their money, chatted with them and gave them change, the words in the letter swirled in my brain, like dust motes in an attic they drifted, forming new clusters and constellations, *wrinkled September timing, uncontainable borderless sheets, Seattle departure suddenly*—and even when I'd finished my shift and read the letter again, even when I'd read it three more times and folded it up and stuffed it in my pocket, even when I'd gone home, climbed up to my room, and put the letter in the bottom drawer of my desk, those words still wouldn't settle.

On the last weekend before school started everyone gathered at the Pier, all kinds of people, kids from other grades and other schools, and someone brought a big tin bucket and filled it with liquor and juice, and someone was selling tabs of acid, and Daniel was filming it all, with the weird confidence he got from wielding his camera he was telling everyone to pose, to say something for the camera, and Inez arrived wearing a shirt she'd ripped the sleeves from and sewn full of zippers, she was insisting we had to do something completely outrageous this year, something the world would never recover from, something that would split open time, crack all the clocks, crush the Reagan administration for good, and Stef and Maeve were pointing at the horizon and trying to get everyone to see that the planet was actually coming closer, getting bigger, any second it was going to explode, any second the world was going to end, and I was there, drunk from the punch like everyone else, saying ridiculous things like everyone else, until suddenly I wasn't—I'd climbed down the ladder and was under the Pier, standing in the mud beneath the Pier. I'd slipped off my shoes, trudged out to where the water started, and let the mud ooze up to my ankles and then to my shins. I liked how compact the mud felt, the thickness of it, my feet claimed by something much bigger than my body, much darker and richer as well, full of squirming and moldering things. Up above the Pier was pulsing and shaking, people were shouting and screeching, pelting each other with words, wounding one another with sounds, but I was down here, my feet sunk in the cool dense silence of the mud. Eventually I climbed back up the ladder, I rejoined everyone else, and when they saw my feet they said, What the fuck happened to you? and I said, Nothing, I was just standing in the mud, and they said, Whatever, Esther, and then we got drunker and someone fell off the Pier and someone punched someone else in the face and then the summer was over.

II

When school started, I had to cut my hours at the bakery in half, by mid-September my savings were gone, and I couldn't afford to pay rent at Paul's. I was so crushed to have to move out that I came back to visit all the time, on Sunday afternoons we'd have tea in his living room, and Paul would fill in another chapter of his life. There was his life as a bouncer on the Lower East Side, his life as a door-to-door salesman, his life as a waiter on cruise ships. He seemed to love all the chapters equally, he narrated even his most miserable moments with the same insatiable charm, the wrinkles around his eyes glinting. Many of the people in his stories had died, his eyes would fill up with tears, his whole face became an overflowing pond, but then with a soft, crinkling laugh he would say, But of course we're all going to die! The opera would soar, Evelyn would chirp her occasional comments, the leaves outside would rustle in the cool autumn wind, and I'd feel, for the suspended hours of those afternoons, completely outside my own life, free from my own narrow frame.

By that time I'd moved in with friends of Monique, two artists named Audrey and Phil, and their six-year-old daughter Ava. They'd offered me the attic room of their dilapidated house in the Central District, the agreement being that I'd cover my rent by babysitting Ava after school, when Audrey was painting at her studio and Phil was still at work. Ava was dreamy and small, with huge dark eyes and olive skin and the uncanny habits of a sleepwalker. She'd appear in my room in the middle of the night, standing by my bed and staring at me, an intensity that wasn't her own intensity peering at me through her eyes. Afternoons we spent playing a game we'd invented, in which she'd whisper in my ear what she really was, and I'd do the same, and then we'd pretend to be normal people, we'd do normal people things, homework and chores, dressing ourselves in human clothes and flossing and brushing our teeth, all the while sending secret signals that hinted at our true hidden selves. The game didn't stop when Audrey and Phil came home, we'd send our signals during dinner, and when Ava went to bed I'd crouch down next to her and whisper that I'd known what she really was the whole time.

I knew Audrey from the theater. She designed the sets and the sound, and worked with Antoine on the lighting, and advised Monique on the staging of scenes. She had a long thin neck and the cavernous eyes of someone who didn't really sleep. When I stayed late she'd drive me home in her beat-up Saab with only one functioning headlight. She drove with a sharp, unpredictable rage, taking a different route up from downtown every night, honking and cursing as she wove through the traffic, hurtling abruptly into turns, biting her nails and shifting gears and talking to me the whole time, about the actors and the play and Monique. They'd worked together for years, had been through everything together, hundreds of plays and losing funding and marriage and childbirth and divorce. I kept my right hand clasped to the door and tucked my left hand under my leg, I told myself it was fine, it would be perfectly fine to die in a spectacular car crash with Audrey, because everything she said was electric: she would slam into a hard right turn and say it was always the men, always the fucking male actors who couldn't get it into their heads that they weren't the stars of the show. All men are egomaniacs, she said, honking at the car in front of her, they're all narcissists, they can't accept the idea that reality isn't organized around them. It had taken Monique *years* to find actors who were willing to take direction from a woman, even some of the *women* wouldn't take direction from a woman, and still even now there were problems: as she accelerated through a yellow light she started talking about all the drama that went on behind the scenes, actors questioning Monique's vision, trying to insert their own pet ideas into the play, and it wasn't like she was a control freak: she genuinely listened to her actors, wanted to hear from them, be in conversation with them—but still, there were the basic principles that made her work her work, that distinguished it from all the other crap out there (there was a lot)—and how many times had she seen men, even the seemingly sensitive ones, sometimes even *especially* those, how many times had she seen them try, over the course of a production, to chip away at those ideas, undermine them? And then you look at what happened with her marriage, she said, slamming the brakes, skidding to a stop inches from the car in front of her, you look at the person her husband became, you see how blind-sided she was by the total monster he turned into, and you can imagine why it's hard for her to trust people. She stopped. We were in the residential streets of the Central District, at a four-way stop, and she turned towards me, her face blue in the light of the dashboard, and I could see a kind of seething just under the tight skin of her cheekbones, a fury her face managed to contain or almost contain. Anyways, she said, as she pulled forward again, she's still going, we're still going.

At home Audrey was a different person, when she stepped out of her car it was like she took leave of herself, her voice when she talked to Phil was flat and fatigued, even with Ava she sounded distant, she often spoke while leaving the room, her words hovering in the space she had just vacated.

—

On a day when I didn't work Jake turned up at the bakery, and I only heard about it later, from one of the bakers, who arched his eyebrow and said, He asked about you. I blushed, my chest filled with heat, my insides churned, my neck muscles spasmed, and all this felt completely out-of-proportion and wrong, because I'd hardly been thinking about Jake at all, not since I'd thrown out his letter, and when I did think about him I usually imagined him dead, he'd plunged through a hole in the ice, he'd starved, he'd been eaten by a bear, his plane had crashed, a crevasse in a glacier had swallowed him up—but the moment the baker said *he asked about you* he resurrected himself in my brain, and my lungs filled with hot scratchy wool that made it impossible to breathe.

He showed up the next day, looking mostly the same, thin and tall, his hair a little longer, his face unfazed as he twisted his rings and said, Hey, and I said, Hey, and then he smirked and said, How's it going? and I shrugged and said, Fine, and he nodded, looked away, and then said he was thinking of maybe seeing a movie tonight, if I felt like coming along, and I said, I don't think there's anything good showing, and he said, Yeah, you're probably right, and then he got a little smile on his face and said, But maybe we could see something bad? I started picking up quarters and dropping them in the bin where the dimes belonged, letting them clink down loudly. I said, I'm not sure I need more bad movies in my life, and then I let another quarter drop, and though I was still looking down I thought I could feel his face flinch a little, his immobile face, with its huge, unblinking eye. He said, Yeah, you're probably right, and then we just stood there silently for a while, and I wondered if he would keep saying *yeah, you're probably right*, again and again, in a loop like the way he twisted his rings, but then he said, We could go for a walk, and I don't know why, I still don't know why but I didn't have a good way to turn down a walk, so I said, Alright, I'm off at five, and he said, Cool, I'll come by.

    We walked through Volunteer Park. I didn't feel like talking about my life, my experiences didn't seem sayable, they were all sealed up inside separate rooms, so when he asked me what I'd been up to I shrugged and said, Nothing much, and then we just walked around the water tower, Jake smoking two cigarettes in a row, until I finally gave in and asked him about Alaska. He said it was alright, he was covered in fish guts most of the time, so nothing really stood out in his memory except the smell of fish. He lifted his arm to his nose and said, I might still smell like a fish. That's great, I said. Eventually we dropped down the back side of Capitol Hill and wound up on a trail through Interlaken, where we had to walk single file, and that was when Jake said, Did you get my letter? He'd started twisting his rings, I could tell by the way his elbows stuck out from his sides, and from their little gyrations I guessed he was twisting them fast. No, I didn't get any letters, I said, hoping he could hear the false note in my voice, wanting him to know that I'd read his letter but wasn't going to acknowledge it, wanting the letter to hang in the air between us like an object I'd stripped the existence from. Oh, he said, I guess it got lost in the mail. I guess so, I said. The trail we were on kept branching, we plunged down into a deep ravine, the forest was thick and dark, and I realized I had no idea where I was, I'd never walked through this park before, I wouldn't have known how to find my way out, and the thought suddenly flashed through my mind that Jake had brought me here to murder me. It was a perfect place for murdering girls. Our bodies would rot right away. I actually thought you were dead, I said abruptly, and he laughed a short soft laugh through his nose and said, Really? Yeah, I said, I imagined you'd died in lots of different ways. Like, you fell into a crevasse and couldn't get out, or you got eaten by a bear. Wow, he said, and I could tell that his hands had frozen, that he was clasping the ring on his middle finger but not twisting it, like his volume control had seized. I wondered if this was the moment when he'd turn around, with a different face, the face he'd always been hiding behind his other face, the face that appeared when his ring system failed, and I'd realize that I'd made my fatal mistake, kept going when I should have turned around. But instead he returned to twisting his rings and said, That's really funny, and I said, Yeah, but what's funnier is still being angry with someone when they're dead.

—

Opening night was a few weeks away, and I was spending all my free time at the theater. I helped Antoine, the lighting guy, with the cues, and washed the costumes at the laundromat down the block, and ran errands at the hardware store for Audrey, and went on coffee runs, and brought day old pastries from the bakery, and posted flyers on telephone poles, and swept the stage, and reorganized the makeup cabinet in the dressing room, and generally did anything anyone needed, anything anyone wanted, plus plenty of things no one needed or wanted at all. At the bakery my days were rote repetitions of other days, indistinguishable from one another, and I zombied my way through my classes at school, my thoughts always elsewhere—I'd be staring at the numbers on the blackboard, when suddenly they'd turn into swimmers, long distance swimmers in the sea, and then I'd hear Inez whispering, *Esther, Esther*, and I'd snap back into consciousness, I'd briefly return to trigonometry, before nodding off again—I was always nodding off and hearing my name again, the dry winds of my whispered name were blowing through the hallways at school, and the thin dust carried by those winds covered everything with a coating of unreality.

 I only woke up at the theater. I loved being surrounded by the actors in the dressing room, getting glimpses into their lives, their intimate lives, the odors of their bodies, the little dances they did as they put on and took off their clothes. They were so at ease with one another's nakedness. There weren't separate rooms for men and women, everyone got dressed and undressed together, and they often hung around in a state in between, wearing only one part of their costumes, the rest of them naked or in everyday clothes, like chimerical creatures from the half-real realm of backstage. They slipped in and out of their characters, each of them contained a whole cosmos of characters they could draw from at any moment, changing their voices and genders, their postures and gestures, even their names. Sometimes I'd join them when they went out to the alley to smoke, and in the darkness, with the high brick walls of the old city looming above us, their faces lit by the glow of their cigarettes became fluid, shape-shifting masks, and dizzy from the nicotine I'd feel myself dissolving into the cackling flames of their laughter, the warm lapping flames of their lives.

When rehearsal was over I'd hang around, waiting for my death ride with Audrey. I'd sweep the stage, or pretend to sweep it while actually just drifting around, feeling how my body felt, how the set made me move, what thoughts and beings it brought out in me. Audrey had built a kind of forest of doors, doors without rooms or walls, just portals scattered in space, like a maze the mind had to imagine for itself, and as I swept or pretended to sweep, I'd make entrances, announcing myself as a different person each time: I was a girl lost in a forest full of wolves, or an amnesiac. I was the silent woman being pursued. I was myself, searching for a bathroom in the halls behind the theater. Or I was no one at all. I hadn't been born yet. I was still deciding which door to enter the world through.

—

And then one night, as I was leaving the theater, Daniel was standing at the bottom of the stairs, filming me as I was coming down, and I paused, I stared straight at his camera, glaring at its undead eye, paralyzed for a moment by its stillness. To my surprise then he put it down, and laughed a little and said, Come on, I'll walk you home, and gestured up the street with a casual flick of his head. His face seemed to have sharpened, become shark-like, his cheekbones now prominent, his skin smooth, as if some inner vacuum had pulled his profile into focus. We started walking up the hill, and I was about to ask him where he'd hidden his friend when he said, So how come we never hang out anymore? There was a smirk in his words, a kind of sarcasm, so I said I didn't know, we both seemed busy, plus frankly his camera wasn't that fun to hang out with. He laughed, then tapped the plastic casing and said, I'm getting some good footage though. Somehow the way he tapped that plastic made me feel like a rat running through a maze for the purpose of some strange experiment. I thought about turning off the street we were on and darting away through an alley, but instead I said, What are you planning to do with it? He smiled a little, then shrugged and said he didn't know, he hadn't decided yet, he was just gathering footage for now, he'd figure out what to do with it later, maybe eventually he'd show it to his dad, it might get worked into his documentary. At some point in that accelerating sentence the anxious energy of some inner urge had gotten the upper hand of him, he'd started walking faster, talking faster, his breathing had quickened and thinned. Will you see him soon? I said, thinking about what Audrey had said, about the total monster his father had turned into, and he said, Yeah, I'm going up there for Christmas. His face had sharpened again, had reassumed its shark-like shape, and with his hands in his pockets he'd started walking with a kind of beat. Cool, was all I said, and then I turned off the street and added, I'm good from here, thanks, and walked away down an alley.

 Later, when I was back in my room, listening to the rain pattering down on the roof, I thought about the time when we'd been close, when we'd all hung around in his living room, me and Daniel and Inez and Maeve, talking about everything, about anything. There had been something sort of endearingly delicate about the way he'd doubted himself back then, retracting everything he said, frantically turning against himself. Now the sound of him tapping his camera was lodged in the back of my brain. Ava walked in with her hair soaking wet, holding two purple thistles by her eyes. Then she ducked out. Waves of rain assaulted the roof. I turned out the light, curled up under the covers, and felt the future ooze like an oil spill into my sleep.

———

For opening night I borrowed a dress from Inez, black, sleeveless, and tight around the neck. It didn't really fit, the chest and the waist were way too loose, but we sort of made it work with a belt. Then Paul cut my hair, short in the back with bangs that hung over my eyes, and Inez did my makeup, cat eyes and crimson lips, and when I stood back from the mirror I felt completely unrecognizable.

We took a cab downtown together. The theater was alive with all the weirdest people of Seattle, all crammed together in the tiny lobby, everyone gorgeous in their own odd way, angular haircuts, dog collars and deconstructed clothes, and as Paul went around greeting the people he knew, which was everyone, Inez on my arm pointed out those she'd have sex with, also everyone, and then the house lights blinked, and I snuck backstage, found Monique in the wings, and gave her a hug. Look at you, she said when she stepped back from me, still holding my shoulders, her eyes reaching into my eyes, and I blushed and said it was Paul's fault, and she laughed and pulled me into the dressing room, where the nerves of the actors were wrinkling in the air, I could smell the rank smell of their sweat, and as Monique moved among them, touching them, holding them, and whispering into their ears, I imagined she was whispering what they really were, the secret of their true hidden selves—and then, for a second, the whole dressing room seemed to coalesce, as everyone drew in their breath, held the air together in their lungs, in one lung, until, breathing out, we broke back into our separate selves, and so I left, went back to find Paul and Inez, and when I sat down Paul pointed to a page in the program, where my name was printed in ink. You're famous, he said.

The house lights dimmed. I don't remember most of the show, my brain was too flooded with emotion, but what struck me was the scene where the silent woman wanders through the forest of doors, while the other actors plot to stab her with daggers. The lights are greenish and low, a whisper of wind skirts over the stage, and there's a sound of fluttering leaves. She drifts around in her slow stunned way, following the flight of some unseen thing, slipping easily away from the sudden lunges of the daggers. She feints and veers, and swerves and ducks, though she's not really trying to avoid them, since she's focused on chasing the thing no one sees. Her pursuers lunge and miss, they lunge and miss again, their faces twisted and leering, their costumes unraveling, and by the end of the scene they've collapsed on the stage and are miserably crawling. The unseen thing flutters offstage, and the silent woman silently follows it.

III

When the show closed, I fell into a funk, a dark slough of indifference and fatigue. I stopped talking to people almost entirely. Even Inez, who'd always been able to get me to do almost anything, often ridiculous, maddening, dangerous things—even she couldn't draw me out of myself, extract me from the murk of myself, my damp, joyless ruminations. I always found some excuse, said I had too much work, was too far behind in school, had to get caught up on things—but the truth was I wasn't getting caught up on anything. I was falling further behind. And further down. I spent most nights just staring at my wall, picking at my skin, writing maudlin entries in my journal.

My house was partly to blame. I'd loved my attic room when I'd first moved in, but it was winter now, a smudge of grey light was all that crept in through the window, the low slanted ceiling was lowering, and when it rained, which was always, the sound of the drops pattering down on the roof seemed to seep into my brain. I could hear Audrey and Phil arguing downstairs, their attempts to keep their voices hushed only making them sound more menacing, all fricatives and rapid-fire sibilants. Eventually Phil would plod up the stairs, go into the room across the hall from mine, and start talking into his machine. His voice was grating and low, like he was scraping clay from the bottom of his being. Meanwhile Audrey would keep roaming around downstairs, her steps like a kind of Morse code I couldn't read.

Work at the bakery had become basically unbearable. I couldn't stand to keep repeating my performance as the girl at the register, the same fake smile over and over again, as if my lips had turned to rubber, and not only my lips, the rubber was spreading to other parts of my body as well, I imagined a future in which the transformation would be complete, and I'd have become a kind of blowup doll, a dummy designed to make the men who walked in feel confident about their choice of muffins.

Jake showed up a few times a week. He'd buy a coffee, chat with the bakers in the back, then sit by the window and pretend to read a sci-fi novel for hours. I kept waiting for one of the bakers to pull him aside, have the conversation guys were supposed to have with other guys, like bro, what you're doing isn't normal, it's kind of creepy actually, let's go shoot some pool—but that never happened, so Jake was allowed to lurk at his table indefinitely, waiting for the bakery to empty out, then launching into long monologues that made no sense to me at all. He said he was thinking of traveling to Mexico and then down into Guatemala and maybe Nicaragua as well. He had a friend who was building a shelter in the jungle in Belize. He thought his housemates were starting to hate him. He wasn't sure why. He'd read somewhere that anyone could become a citizen of the Dominican Republic. Pretty much everything was made out of corn these days, which our digestive systems weren't adapted to. Our civilization was definitely in decline. Only Eskimos would survive the apocalypse. The rest of us were going to die.

One day I'd gone to the bathroom at the end of my shift, and came back to find Jake standing in the middle of the space, marooned in a kind of no man's land between the tables and chairs, staring at his fingers as he twisted his rings. Something about his face was wrong, the way his features slid away from one another, went slack, his whale eye swimming awkwardly inside its socket. He looked up at me for a second, then down again at his rings, twisting them one way and the other, as if they'd lost their grip on whatever they'd once been connected to, like nuts on a bolt from which all the grooves had been stripped.

—

I still went down to the theater every once in a while, when I had an afternoon off. There was no reason to go, the theater was closed, our funding had been cut after a journalist had called our play obscene, all because of one little scene in which Anne had appeared naked. The stage was stark and stripped down. We'd struck the set a couple days after the show closed, so the forest of doors was now a clear cut. A pile of two-by-fours sat by the fire exit. The dressing room was a mess, costumes lying around, empty champagne bottles, ashtrays full of cigarette butts, props, takeout boxes, wigs like the carcasses of dead animals dangling over the backs of chairs. I'd walk out to the stage and then down into the rows of empty seats, where I'd sit in the spot where I'd watched all the shows. I'd stare down the empty stage, mentally remaking the set and the lights and the sound, craving the moment when the curtain opened.

Later I'd go to the arcade on second and waste my money playing Pac-Man. I wasn't good at it. My strategy was to sit by the power pellets and wait for the ghosts to approach, then devour them in a frenzy of aggression. But I usually went too far, kept hunting them down even when they began to blink, and got eaten by them instead.

—

I went to see Monique. I hadn't seen her since the show closed, mostly because I was avoiding Daniel, but I was also a little haunted by the thought that I'd embarrassed myself at the cast party. I'd blacked out. Audrey had apparently taken me home. I'd woken in the morning with a steel spike splitting my brain and the vague sensation that I might have done something mortifying. The last thing I remember was sitting on the couch next to Anne, trying to tell her how much her performances had meant to me. The night plunged off a cliff after that. I'd spent the next day in bed, puking every time I'd tried to stand up, dredging the void where the rest of the night should have been.

To my relief, Monique seemed happy to see me. She gave me a hug, then preempted my attempts to apologize with a casual wave of her hand. We've all had a few bad cast parties, she said. She seemed strangely at ease for someone whose whole reason for being had just been annihilated by Reagan. We sat in her living room, among her books and records and plants, the eternal smell of earl grey tea. When she leaned towards me and said, How *are* you? it was like she was staring into places even I didn't have access to—and I felt, for a moment, something loosen inside me, some tangle of nerves seemed to be untangling itself, I was about to release a whole flood of feelings when the sound of someone coming into the kitchen interrupted me, footsteps and a jangling of keys, Monique raised her head and said, Marcus? Is that you? Come meet Esther, and then a tall thin man, with an angular face and a chin fringed with stubble, sauntered into the room, settled into the armchair across from me, and said, Hello.

I didn't understand how someone I'd never seen in this house could suddenly establish such a familiar relation to the furniture. There was something insectile, something even a little predatory about the way he sat in the chair, his long thin legs tightly crossed, his fingers pressed together in front of his mouth, pulsing slightly, like a praying mantis preparing to ambush its prey. Monique said he was a writer and a director, that he'd worked in New York and met Beckett and Pinter and was currently at work on a new play. You'd *love* his work, she said. Are you an actor? he said, a question that took me aback, I'm not sure why, somehow the directness of it felt shattering, I stuttered something about helping out with this and that, and then Monique came to my rescue and said, Esther does a little bit of everything. Ah, he said, in a soft, easy, obliterating way, like he was stepping on one of those mushrooms that's nothing but dust.

I didn't stay long. It was perfectly clear that the praying mantis was eager for me to leave, so that he could stun Monique with his poisonous proboscis and drag her back to his lair with the rest of his prey. I walked down to the Pier, thinking the mud might suffocate my memory, which kept spitting up chunks I couldn't swallow down. Worst of all had been the way Monique had looked at him, the admiration in her eyes, their gelatinous softness, her irises jiggling like the yolks of raw eggs. At the Pier I climbed down the ladder, removed my shoes, and waded out, feeling the mud ooze between my toes. I wanted to sink all the way down, until the mud encased my thigh bones and rib bones and breasts, clogged up my nose and mouth, sealing me up in the silence of clay.

—

I finally gave into Inez. She'd been relentless in her attempts to resuscitate Esther the Dead, as she'd started calling me, when she rang me at night, saying, Oh, sorry, I must have dialed the wrong number, I was looking for the living Esther, but it sounds like I've reached Esther the Dead—a routine that had become so intolerable that I finally gave in out of spite. We took the bus to a party at a huge house in Laurelhurst. People were playing drinking games and making out in the halls, they were shouting at one another to drink, and hurling themselves into the pool, everyone exploding and splattering. I started slurping down drinks, trying to get drunk as fast as I could, to blur the edges of things, smear the features of faces, my own face as well, but for some reason the alcohol seemed to have no effect on me. Inez got trapped talking to a boy, so I snuck upstairs alone, amazed by the silence of my footsteps on the carpeted stairs. I felt weightless, imperceptible. I was floating upwards without any effort at all, almost like I didn't exist. I slipped into a walk-in closet and started feeling all the clothes, obliterating my face in that kelp forest of sumptuous textures. The next thing I knew I was wearing a black dinner jacket, I'd rolled up the sleeves and was looking at myself in the floor length mirror, my body now big and box-like, my shoulders angular and broad, something jutting and sheer about the figure in the mirror staring back at me.

Back downstairs, Inez's eyes flared when she saw me. She turned to the boy she was with and said, Matt, meet my friend *Carla*. This is Carla. Hi Carla, said Matt. He told us he knew about a much better party, so we followed him out to his car. I sat in the back, the window rolled down, watching the city rush by like a sci-fi film, all velocity and streaks of bright light. The wind on my face brought my crime into focus, helped me separate it, isolate it, claim it as an act I'd actually committed instead of just another dumb thing that had happened to me. I wondered if that was true. I wondered how many things in my life I could really call mine. We went to a bunch of other parties that night, getting drunker and drunker each time. I hardly remember the last two. Someone cracked their head against the edge of a coffee table. Inez made out with a guy.

—

And then one night, just before winter break, we saw Daniel at a party we regretted going to the moment we walked through the door, the air inside thick with skin cells and swamp water and dread, a rank, heavy, glandular smell saturating everything. A bunch of boys sat hunched like gargoyles on the couches, Daniel among them, their eyes stitched in a zombified stare to the television, where a shaky close-up showed the face of a man struggling to breathe, his eyes bulging with astonishment. Daniel's friend stood behind the couches, presiding over the scene, his gaunt face immobile, frozen like the surface of some distant moon, and I felt like he wasn't watching the footage so much as watching the others watch the footage, silently commanding them to maintain the intensity of their attention. They hadn't looked up when we came in, hadn't even glanced in our direction, had kept their eyes unswervingly on the grainy close-up of the man, who I now realized was being strangled. I don't know what held us there, why we didn't leave, turn around immediately and leave, why we watched on, our bodies leaden and numb, stunned into astonishment like the man being strangled, our faces throbbing and inflamed. It wasn't until the last breath of life was choked out of the man that Inez said, *Let's get out of here*, and turned towards the door, and I looked at Daniel, saw that he was looking at me, his eyelids low, the energy that usually lived in his face drained away.

—

When winter break came, I went back to riding buses around town, sitting for hours at my favorite cafes, wearing my black dinner jacket with the sleeves rolled up over a ratty t-shirt or sweater. I'd started writing a story. It was about a girl named Emilia, who lived in a room where the light was always on, because she was afraid of the dark. She owned a doll named Esther the Dead, which she kept in a box in the bottom drawer of her dresser. Every night, before she went to bed, she'd take Esther out of her box, and stab her with pins, and twist off her head, and tell her what a stupid fucking loser she was, and accuse her of being ugly and dead. On Sundays, Emilia would lunch with her grandmother at the club, where her grandmother would teach her how to be a lady. A *lady*, her grandmother would say, with breath that smelled of bitterness and money, must always order steak. And the steak must always be rare, very rare. But, she must never eat more than one bite of it. Just the smallest little morsel, no more. Then she should smile, and lean over the table towards her husband, and slide her plate very slowly towards him. *That*, she concluded, was how to be a lady.

After lunch, Emilia would ride home in her grandmother's silver Mercedes. It was the highlight of her whole week. With her seatbelt buckled and her hands clasped tightly in her lap, she knew she'd always be enshrined in nice things. Hadn't her ballet teacher, Ms. Ratmonovich, said something similar? She'd wrapped her knuckles on the hard bones of Emilia's remarkable ribcage, and said, This is your jewel box, my dear. Inside it live precious jewels. You mustn't ever cover them in fat!

But I couldn't finish the story. I wrote a bunch of versions and wound up hating them all. I wrote one where Emilia has a psychotic breakdown at prom, and has to be hauled away in an ambulance. I wrote another where Esther returns from the land of the dead, now a huge, half-plastic cyborg, and eats Emilia's head like a lollipop. In the last one I wrote, Emilia turns sixteen, and gets her driver's license, and as a gift, her grandmother lets her drive them home in the silver Mercedes—but Emilia loses control, and swerves into onrushing traffic, killing both of them instantly. All of these versions were bad, so I stuffed the story in the bottom drawer of my dresser, where Esther the Dead apparently belonged.

—

I went home for Christmas. My parents had decided the issue was non-negotiable. They would pick me up on Christmas Eve, we would have dinner together, I would stay the night, and then we'd all get up on Christmas morning, eat cinnamon rolls and open presents, as we'd always done in the past. That was the plan. It wasn't what happened. Over dinner I announced that I wasn't applying to college. My father's face did something I'd never seen it do before, his cheeks inflating like a puffer-fish, while my mother's lower jaw jut forward and froze, her tiny nostrils flared, she sucked in some air and said, You're ruining yourself, you're intentionally destroying yourself just to prove some kind of point. I stormed upstairs and slammed the door behind me. I hardly slept that night, but when I did nod off, I dreamed that the walls of my room were pressing towards me, closing in on me, like in that trash compactor scene from *Star Wars*. I left in the morning before my parents woke up and walked down to the bus stop. Of course it was Christmas and there weren't any buses, so I hitched a ride with a friendly old man who looked like someone's dead uncle. He dropped me off at the Montlake exit. I walked up the hill, my nerve ends stinging in the breeze. No one was home in my house. I went up to my attic room, put my headphones on and crawled under the covers.

—

For New Year's Eve, Monique was throwing a party, and she'd invited everyone from the cast and crew of the play. I hadn't seen most of them since the cast party, and I imagined that night was the only thing they remembered about me, everything else had probably been blotted out by whatever I'd done at the party, and who even knew what that was, I still couldn't remember, I might have puked in someone's lap, or tried to make out with one of the actors, or puked in the lap of the actor I was trying to make out with.

Fortunately everyone was warm, the actors all gave me hugs, Monique was in the kitchen assembling some snacks with Audrey, and they both came together to embrace me at the same time, one on each side, and then Monique ran a hand down the lapel of my dinner jacket and said, You look absolutely ravishing in this, before mentioning a little project she had in mind for me, having something to do with a grant she was writing, she'd explain more later, was I interested? I said of course, of course I said of course, I'd be happy to do anything or everything, and did this mean the theater would be opening again soon? We'll see, said Monique, lifting her brows, breathing in, and then holding that breath high in her chest, before turning to Audrey, who looked back at her with an expression so full of years, so textured with depths of knowing, that I thought, No one will ever know me that well, ever.

I behaved very well at the party. I only had two glasses of champagne, and managed a normal, even somewhat boring conversation with Anne, about vegetarianism, and joked with Antoine about his bad luck with girls, and smoked a cigarette with Audrey in the backyard, and generally conducted myself in an extremely respectable and adult manner for the entirety of the night, then left before midnight to meet Inez. There was only one bad moment, right before I left, when I came back inside after smoking with Audrey, and saw the praying mantis sitting in his chair, his legs tightly crossed, his eyes fixed in an immobile stare, the tips of his fingers pressed together and pulsing.

—

Winter kept seeping into everything, like some clammy dead hand from a horror film. Ava seemed to feel it as well. I'd noticed the way she moved through the house, sliding with her back against the walls, stepping around spaces in the kitchen, giving an extra-wide birth to the coffee table. When I asked her what this was about, she told me she was avoiding the wet spots. They were everywhere, she said. Sometimes she'd grab my wrist suddenly, tug me back, her fingernails pressing into my skin. It's wet, she'd say, her face hard and fixed, her eyes lit with some dark liquid squeezed from her nights full of dreams. Eventually she showed me all the spots, there, and there and there, and there's a new one there, and this one's getting bigger, and I made sure to avoid them as we walked, I stepped over them as well, and started doing this even when I was alone, as a game, knowing it wasn't a game, it was something I also felt, something I was beginning to feel, the moisture seeping through the floorboards, the wet spots invading the walls.

And then one day Audrey came into my room and asked me to help her do the shopping. We got in her car, but rather than drive directly to the store, she patched together an erratic puzzle of side streets, surging forward and stopping, hurtling into turns, slamming the breaks at four way stops, and talking to me the whole time, about how Phil had become a black hole, his obsession with himself all-consuming. He finds his own personal psychodrama so utterly absorbing that he can't understand that I don't always have time for it. He's actually *offended* by the fact that I'm not emotionally available to him twenty-four hours a day, that I don't voluntarily *hurl* myself into the seething pit of his self-loathing and shame. I should apparently put aside my career, not to mention my *own* emotional needs, whenever his fear of failure flares up. The whole fucking world could be on fire and Phil would still think that his personal problems were more important. Actual things that happen in *reality* are somehow less pressing than the trivial developments of his inner life. I mean, the NEA cuts our funding on the basis of an article written by some total hack, and what does Phil have to say about it? *You'll bounce back, you always do*, that's it, end of discussion, now let's turn to the real breaking news, which is that Phil is feeling that he might be a failure. He'll get this dead look in his eyes and say, I feel like a failure. And he'll expect me to pull him out of this pit he's fallen into for like the *two hundredth time*, he'll expect me to stop whatever I'm doing and haul him out of this pit, which, by the way, he's dug *for himself*. You'd think that maybe having dug the pit he'd know how to avoid falling into it, but no, he falls into his own fucking pit, or maybe intentionally *throws* himself into it, like some eight year old desperate for attention, exactly like that in fact, and then I have to drop whatever I'm doing and spend the next several hours, and sometimes the next several *days*, hauling him out of it, while also, of course, doing everything else. It's exhausting. It's fucking *infuriating*. I'm not sure how much longer I can stand it.

In the end, we didn't wind up at the grocery store, but at Audrey's studio. She seemed somewhat surprised by this herself, as if someone else had been driving the car. She invited me to come in anyways. I'd never seen her paintings, only the work she'd done for the theater, but they were similar: her huge, white-washed canvases looked a little like the forest of doors, abstract spaces with suggestions of slots you could pass through, hints of windows, cracks between walls, symbols that looked like exit signs, though where the exits were wasn't clear. I walked around, her words still buzzing through my brain, until Audrey came up beside me and looked at the canvasses with me for a while. We never did do the shopping.

IV

School started again, my last semester of high school, and it felt more purposeless and vapid than all the other semesters combined, though everyone said this semester was actually the most meaningful, *our last semester of high school*, as if being the last somehow made something significant, as if the middles of things had no significance at all, only the beginnings and ends. I ghosted my way through my classes, not paying attention to anything, doodling in my sketchbook, listening to the sound of the rain falling or the branches rattling in the wind. I even spaced out in my English class, the only class I usually paid attention to, because we were reading *Great Expectations*, a novel I loathed. I took revenge on the book by mangling its sentences, cutting them up and mashing them together, making new combinations that amused me: *my father was a bleak place overgrown with nettles; nothing regarding my mother was freckled; the identity of things derived from the lair from which the savage wind was blowing.*

Luckily I now had work at the theater. For the grant she was writing, Monique had to tell the story of the company, so she'd asked me to organize the archive, which wasn't really an archive at all, just a bunch of boxes shoved under the desk in the theater office, stuffed full of scripts and photographs and notebooks and sketches and newspaper clippings and props, all thrown together with no apparent order at all. I wasn't sure why she'd asked me, of all people, to help her, I knew nothing of the history of the company, I suspected she was only being nice to me, providing some purpose when I seemed to have none, but regardless I loved the work, and stayed up late sorting through the boxes, making piles that belonged to each play. The variety of worlds the company had created was astonishing, there were plays with enormous puppets, one where the actors were suspended from wires, and another in which three talking heads sprouted from the rims of huge urns. It struck me as sort of absurd, but also beautiful, beautifully absurd, that they'd built all these fantastical worlds only to break them down a few weeks later, and that the only remaining trace of them, the only evidence they'd even existed, was stuffed in a few cardboard boxes in the theater office. I spent hours reading notes Monique had written in the margins of scripts, studying Audrey's sketches for sets, and staring at photographs of productions from the early days of the company, in the mid-seventies, when Monique and Audrey were both so young, so ecstatic and ferocious, their faces possessed, their eyes alive with an otherworldly energy. The productions in those early days looked savage, naked people covered in paint, crawling like reptiles on the stage, actors captured with their mouths torn open by screams.

It was a strange time to be in the office. The later I stayed, the more I heard the slurred shouting of drunk men spilling out of bars, the lunatic ravings of the homeless, and the hushed voices of people lined up in the halls behind the dressing room. Sometimes I'd rest my head on the desk and drift off into eerie dreams. I dreamed that the theater was filling up with foam. I dreamed that Anne was a mouse who could sing.

And then one night while sorting through the archive I came across a photograph of Marcus. He was standing on the stage with Monique, his hands out in front of him, shaping something in the air, while Monique was standing beside him, looking up at him. At the back of the stage Audrey was looking on, one hand clasped to her clavicle, the other gripping her wrist, her face narrowed and drawn. I folded that photograph in half, folded it again, stashed it in the inner pocket of my dinner jacket, and then, on my way home, threw it in the trash.

—

I still saw Daniel at school, since we were in the same science class, and I crossed him in the halls and ran into him in the cafeteria, but he kept avoiding eye contact with me. Ever since he'd returned from Montreal he'd decided I didn't exist. Part of me was relieved, I found him unbearable after all, the way he tracked me down with the bludgeoning eye of his camera, the way he hid his timidity behind that illegible machine, substituted its dead cyclops eye for his own, though another part felt like this new refusal was extreme, even violent. You couldn't just decide someone didn't exist. You couldn't just edit them out of your reality. In the dining hall he'd started sitting with a new group of friends, all boys, their faces only half-formed, like they'd just been made, the finishing touches still missing, and I noticed the way they looked at him, with a kind of absorption just short of awe, as if Daniel's aloofness had consolidated the inner substance of him, made him more dense, and these smaller planets had been sucked into his orbit. His cheeks had flattened, become slab-like and blue, and his shoulders looked locked into place like sentinels guarding both sides of him. He'd started walking in a new way too, with a bit of a limp, maybe it was caused by the camera equipment he perpetually carried around with him, but he seemed to exaggerate it, play it up, adding a strut or a lope to his limp.

Inez thought he hated us because we knew him too well. She was walking me to work after school one day when she spelled out her whole theory of him. We should be in some kind of witness protection program, actually, she said. Because that's what we are, witnesses to the person he used to be. No one will believe in the new Daniel if the memory of the old one is still around. And we're the memory. We keep the old Daniel alive. So basically he's hunting that memory down like some kind of assassin.

During my shift that day, while dishing slices of banana bread and dealing out blueberry muffins, I imagined a new version of my story, in which Emilia goes on a killing spree, assassinating all her friends. She finds them in the corner of her closet, all shapeless and covered with lint, like a litter of newborn mice. She slips little bags over their heads, then stuffs their breathless bodies into a box. Snapping the lid shut, she feels radiant, perfect, and clean, her face burning like a fluorescent bulb, like a light so white it blacks out the past.

—

I went to see Paul. For a long time I'd been wondering if the adults in my life loved me or actually just tolerated me, whether secretly they saw me as a burden, a liability, this teenager who got too drunk at their parties and clung too desperately to the edges of their lives, but for some reason that worry didn't infect my friendship with Paul, who immediately reprimanded me for not having visited him for a month, and told me my hair looked horrible, and whisked me into his kitchen and set up a chair, threw a towel over my shoulders, and went to work with his scissors, snipping away, all the while demanding that I tell him everything, absolutely everything that was happening in my life. I told him about the closure of the theater and my fears that my house was falling apart, about the archive and Jake and the appalling Christmas I'd spent with my parents, and felt all of these bits of trivial drama dissolve upon contact with Paul. It was a rainy afternoon, but his house still felt luminous, as if the light bloomed from the old wooden floors, with the single exception of a thick line of shadow hovering under the door of my room. I still thought of that room as mine, my memories of living there were still so vivid, those afternoons when the sun came in filtered through the maple leaves. Of course I'd met Paul's new roommate, an extremely friendly person named Kevin, and accepted the fact that the room was now his, especially since he'd always left the door open, as if inviting my memories in.

But now it was closed. Somehow I sensed that Kevin was there, despite the dark line under the door. Paul talked about taking Evelyn to the vet, about the new man he was dating, about the way time seemed to pass so quickly when your life settled down, but eventually I sensed he was avoiding something, very nimbly stepping around the edges of something, his conversation growing more vague. When he finished my hair and swept up the clippings and we were sitting on his couch sipping tea, the wrinkles radiating around his eyes seemed to sag. Evelyn chirped, the voice of the opera singer soared, but the bar of shadow under my door only thickened.

—

And then my big chance arrived, one night while I was working at the theater, and I didn't seize it at all. Monique had started offering workshops in the evenings, not just for actors but for anyone, and sometimes while I was sorting through the archive these workshops would be going on, and I'd take a break and sneak into a seat and watch Monique at work with a group of adults. She told them what she thought acting really was, and more importantly what it wasn't. Acting for me isn't about speaking your lines, she said, it isn't even about getting into character. So-called real life is much more like that kind of acting. We're all acting all the time, saying what people expect us to say, being who people expect us to be. We get into character in the same way we get dressed. So a lot of what we're going to do here will be about getting *out* of character. We're going to have to stop being ourselves.

First she asked everyone to make up a gesture. It couldn't be a gesture we would understand. This is going to sound strange, she said, but I don't want you to try to *communicate*. You're not trying to tell us something. I'm asking you to make your body do something it's never done before. You don't need to know what it means. In fact, you shouldn't know what it means. Then, as people began twisting and contorting their hands, making shapes with their fingers, angling their arms, Monique moved among them, not touching them but coming close to them, occasionally offering suggestions. Maybe move on from your hands, she would say. Our hands are too well trained. And when she spoke to one person, her words would create a kind of ripple effect through the rest, hips and knees and ankles would begin to move, and a sort of rhythmless dance of discombobulated bodies would take shape on the stage.

One night she asked me if I'd like to join. She appeared at the door of the theater office, a kind of conspiratorial smile on her lips, and said, You're welcome to join us tonight, Esther, we'll be starting in a few minutes. I was so conditioned to say yes to Monique, to say yes immediately and automatically, no matter what she was offering or asking me to do, that I said yes to this too, my mouth simply made the motions of yes, I'd love to, thank you, and then a couple minutes later I found myself standing on the stage, in my socks, surrounded by a bunch of adults, feeling like my organs were about to explode. I hadn't realized how terrifying it was to do what Monique was asking us to do, to stand there more or less naked, in a circle of people I didn't even know—and once everyone started to move, using their bodies in the way Monique was instructing us to use them, becoming alien to themselves, and to one another, I simply froze. I remembered watching the actors doing their warm-ups, the way they birthed themselves into completely new bodies on the stage, but I was stillborn, and could only stand there staring at the others, their bodies all contorted and wrong, their gestures lurid and deranged. I looked around in horror and dismay, until, in a moment when Monique had her back turned to me, I snuck offstage.

—

I don't know what happened to time after that, it seemed to stall, to get stuck in the pattern of unchanging weather, every day the same ceaseless drizzle, a monotony of clouds eclipsing the sky, the Seattle winter holding the sun hostage, holding the whole idea of change hostage, every day repeating other days. Walking home through the park I started thinking about those planted forests where every tree is the same, forests like matrices, like grids. The forest was school and work and getting up and going to bed and taking people's money and giving them change, the forest was the city with its sidewalks chopped into blocks, and it didn't matter whether the earth was flat or round, whether the sun revolved around the earth, or the earth around the sun, because the weather never changed, and the only evidence that time was passing was the fact that I was getting wetter.

To get revenge on that block of weather and time I started stealing more things. On the weekends I'd go to parties with Maeve and Inez, any kind of party at all, parties of hippies or preppies, parties of punks and goths, frat parties. I'd get drunk and shrink down, it was a special talent I had, becoming smaller when drunk. I hardly made any sound, I'd sneak into bedrooms upstairs, or find a moment when the kitchen was empty, and I'd spy some small, unimportant object, a refrigerator magnet, a tea cozy, a paper weight, a comb, and stash it in the inside pocket of my dinner jacket. I didn't care much about the objects themselves, it was more about the act, about marking time, making a dent in time or a gash. I kept the objects on the desk in my room, and arranged them in the order in which I'd stolen them, my little calendar of purloined things.

I also quit my job. I hadn't planned on it, in fact I'd planned on working even more, to make as much money as I could, so that when summer came I could travel somewhere, Canada or California, France or Japan, but then one day a customer complained that his banana nut muffin was dry, he insisted I'd given him a day old muffin while charging the regular price, he wanted a refund and another muffin. I just stared at his face, his cheeks the color of pork chops, his eyes small and grey, and then I said, Great, returned his money, took the muffin back from him, and crumbled it into the register.

I started riding buses to the ends of their lines. I was disappointed to discover that the ends of bus lines weren't actually interesting places. In fact they weren't really places at all, just anonymous nowheres, parking lots surrounded by buildings whose facades refuted all hope of intrigue. I kept traveling to those places anyways, staring out the window with my headphones on, imagining new versions of my story. There was one where Esther the Dead arrives at the theater, now closed for many years, the walls covered with water stains, the ceiling crumbling. For months she wanders the warren of halls, and when one night she opens a door, and the man with the heavy eyelids says, You here for an audition? she says, Yes, yes I am.

—

And then one day at school I saw a flyer posted in the halls, announcing the screening of Daniel's film. It was called *Rat Trap*. I showed the flyer to Inez, who couldn't get over how pretentious it was. I mean, 'written and directed by Daniel Tremblay'? she said. Who the fuck does he think he is?

The screening took place on a Friday afternoon, in a small basement room at school. Inez and Maeve and I showed up together, dressed for the occasion in our shittiest clothes, big flannel shirts and shredded jeans, ruined Converse high tops, studded belts. We sat in the back, the only girls in the room. The boys with unfinished faces were there, plus Daniel's imaginary friend, who stood in a back corner by himself. A dank smell of hormonal excitement filled the already dank room. Daniel didn't say anything about his film, didn't acknowledge his audience, didn't even seem to want to be present in the room—he just killed the lights, crouched down by the VCR, and pushed play.

It wasn't really a film, just a collage of footage Daniel had taken of people at parties and at the Pier, all close-ups, excruciatingly close, you could see the pores in people's skin, their pimples and blackheads, their scars. He'd asked everyone to pose, to say something to the camera, but the film didn't include anything they'd said or even the figures they'd struck, only the moments afterwards, when they couldn't tell if the camera was filming or not, and their faces stumbled, got stuck in between two expressions, seemed to slip for a moment outside the form their personalities tried to impose on them—and Daniel had honed in on those moments, slowed them down, accentuating every contortion of lips, every crease that crumpled a chin, every string of saliva strung between teeth. I thought of the footage the boys had been watching at the party, the close-up of the man being strangled, and I felt like Daniel was attacking our faces, mangling and destroying them, his camera an insatiable maw. I wasn't surprised when I saw my own face, though it took me a while to see it as mine. My lips looked like they were about to fall off my mouth, my eyes rolled around in my head, and a thread of vomit dangled from my chin.

We left the moment the film ended. We filed out of that room in the basement of the school as the credits rolled on the screen, credits that only credited Daniel, in a kind of sick repetition, cinematography by Daniel Tremblay, editing by Daniel Tremblay, soundtrack by Daniel Tremblay, written by Daniel Tremblay, directed by Daniel Tremblay, a film by Daniel Tremblay.

V

When summer came, Inez and I abandoned the idea of buying a car. We'd been talking a lot about cars, before school was even over we'd discussed the subject endlessly, what kind of car we would buy, which tapes we'd bring on our trips, whether we'd go to L.A. or Chicago first, New York or New Orleans first. Of course we were both broke, our meager paychecks mostly devoured by clothes and booze and caffeine. At one point we made some calculations, figured that if we led boring, sober, fashionless lives for two months, we could save enough money to buy a car, a crappy used car that might get us as far as Tacoma before it gave out. But what was the point, by then it would already be August, the earth all burnt, the sky a brown wash, the best days of summer gone by.

Instead we took the bus downtown to the International District, to the big thrift store with the bins, where you could buy clothes by the pound. We battled the crowds that swarmed those bins and pulled things out of them almost randomly. Back at Inez's we cut sleeves off shirts and sewed them onto the shoulders of other shirts, we scissored jeans in half, and stitched them together with the halves of other jeans, and sewed zippers into the thighs, made shirts that zipped up the sides, the stitches jagged and showing. Inez didn't care if the clothes she made fell apart. If people actually started wearing these things, she said, they wouldn't last long either. Most of them would actually just die. They would have aneurisms or something. It would be like population thinning through fashion.

Later we'd go down to the Pier. Over the winter the city had tried to shut it down, they'd erected a fence across it, and hung a sign warning that trespassing was not only illegal but potentially fatal, that violators would be prosecuted, electrocuted, decapitated, and fined, but all we had to do was attach a rope to the top of one of the posts, grab the rope and swing around. Then we'd sit on the end of the Pier and talk about our plans for the future. Obviously Inez was going to be a fashion designer, and I was going to start a theater company, and we imagined collaborations where my actors would wear her designs. Opening night would be the launch of her new line, her clothes that would actually kill people.

Some nights Stef and Maeve would show up, and they'd drag along other friends, and soon the Pier would be packed with people, people we knew and didn't know, all of them more or less like us, just graduated from high school, relieved to be done with it all, terrified to be done with it all, exhausted, ecstatic, voracious, confused. Eventually the pilings would start to shake, the rotting wooden boards would begin to bend, and I'd imagine that one night, when we were drunk and our silhouettes were exploding against the night sky, those boards would buckle and the pilings would break and we'd all plunge in one mangled mass into the mud down below.

—

By then I'd found a job at a used bookstore on 15th. The owner had apparently taken the bait on my resumé, in which I'd made the work I'd done for Monique sound far more impressive than it was, especially since that work had come to nothing. He was a bearded dyspeptic behemoth of a man who brooded over his kingdom of books like some kind of mythical giant. He hardly ever moved from his desk, he seemed to have fused with it physically, and he inspected the books people brought in with suspicion and boredom and disdain, his lips burbling words or not even words, just random orderings of letters, like a lava flow of non-language. He'd hired me to organize the shelves in the back of his shop, where there was no system at all, just books stacked on top of other books, books hidden behind other books, towers of books like termite nests rising from the warped wooden floors. I'd sit cross-legged on the floor in that dusty back room, picking up books from one stack, reading a page, then putting them down in another stack. It seemed likely that I'd die from dust inhalation before making any progress at all, or I'd faint one day and when I came back to I'd find myself gagged and bound, the bones of previous employees scattered all around my feet. But I actually did like the work, reading bits of books all day, often in the company of Charles, the huge orange cat who lounged and prowled around the shop. Every once in a while a customer would come in, and I'd ask if I could help them find anything, but for the most part I was alone, free to drift in my own small universe of thought.

    After work I'd walk around the neighborhood, surprised to discover that the world still existed. I liked my citadel of words, but it was a relief to be reminded that there were also things, real things with thickness and color, people, houses, sidewalks, trees. I'd walk through the park and stare up at the leaves of the maples, feeling dizzy and a little overwhelmed, like I'd only just been born.

—

I'd also apprenticed myself to Audrey. A company she had no respect for had commissioned her to design and build the set for a play she detested, and she'd agreed, needing the money, though she admitted that she actually liked this kind of work, it was easy for her, it freed up some part of her brain. The set for the play was supposed to look real, a real house with real rooms and furniture, and the actors were supposed to say and do real things. I don't see the point of it, said Audrey. I liked watching her work, the spidery quickness of her body, her thin muscled arms, the way her eyes drew lines on whatever they looked at. She taught me how to use her tools, tools capable of truly terrifying things, things only aliens or gods should be capable of. Eventually she gave me small projects, parts of the set that wouldn't show, and though I messed up everything seventeen times I felt proud, stupidly proud of even my smallest accomplishments.

Sometimes people from the theater would stop by, Antoine and Anne, a few other actors, and they'd go outside to smoke and laugh about their lives, the shitty gigs they had lined up for the summer, how the director was a total creep, the costumes were embarrassing, the pay was shit, the hours were abominable, the other actors were assholes, the dressing room stank, the stage was rotting, they bused the entire audience in from nursing homes. People snore, said Anne. There's a lot of snoring.

—

And since Daniel had gone back to Montreal, a curse had been lifted, a spell dispelled, Monique's house was completely free of all his creepy equipment, and I could go over there again, I could sit with her in her living room, surrounded by her books and her records, her paintings and plants, and talk about the future of the theater, what she imagined for upcoming plays, she was confident they'd eventually find funding, they always had in the past, she'd been rereading Aeschylus, Sartre, Gombrowicz and Artaud, and going to see a lot of dance, she'd always been fascinated by the work of Martha Graham, her tragedies especially, what she'd done with Clytemnestra was astonishing—and then she rose from the couch, as if everything she'd said had been building up to that movement, which she accomplished with such seamless ease, such insouciance, and while drifting towards the kitchen she said, Would you like another cup of tea, Esther? and I said, Yes, yes please.

And so, at the bookstore, I began compiling a shelf with all the names Monique had mentioned, all those names and more, I scoured the store for anything to do with Greek tragedy and dance, with Martha Graham and Aeschylus, and I found scholarly books and monographs and different translations of the plays, plus writers associated with the others she'd named, and I organized the shelf so that the spines of these books looked stately but also esoteric, serious but also arcane, and imagined the day when Monique would come in and I'd show her the shelf I'd made for her, like a gift to her, or a shrine. Of course I also read the books in my own time, devouring them with such hunger and speed that the misery of Audrey arguing with Phil rarely entered my consciousness—and while reading I imagined the sets Audrey and I would design, houses that clicked like discordant clocks, rooms within rooms like Russian dolls, and enchanted forests where the silver leaves would quiver without any wind. I hardly slept at all in those days, my window was open all the time, and the smells that wafted in on the breeze filled me with wordless yearnings.

—

Sometimes Ava would climb into my bed, woken by her bad dreams. Summer hadn't cleared up the wet spot problem in our house, if anything she was seeing more of them, and her face had grown blotchy, dark patches blooming on her forehead and cheeks, her skin like a map of the gloomy moods in the house. During the day I took her outside whenever I could, dragged her along on my rambles through the city. We rode buses together to random neighborhoods and stopped for snacks at cafes, and in the parks we lay down under trees, and played a game where she would ask me how old I was, and I would say, I'm at least a hundred and twenty years old, and she would say, I'm five hundred and seventeen! and I would say, I'm seven hundred and thirty-five! and then we'd stare at the sky, seeing who could look the oldest, who could think the most ancient thoughts. Ava's oldest thoughts were questions, like why didn't people have wings, and why were there girls and boys, not just one kind of person, and why did humans live in houses, and were there children that didn't have parents, and why did most children have two parents instead of three or sixteen? I said I didn't know, things just were the way they were, someone had decided that's how it was and a bunch of other people had agreed. I don't think she liked my answers, but I was relieved at least to see that her eyes in these moments looked bright and alert and a little wild, unclouded by her dreams or rather clouded by better dreams.

Back at home her face hardened again, her eyes scanned the floor, she took a step and then stopped, a step and then stopped, as if the house would collapse if she touched the wrong spot.

—

And then one day Monique told me she was going away, she was leaving in a week, to work with Marcus on his play, which was set to open in New York in September. It was such an exciting opportunity, she said, such a rare and exciting opportunity to work with an artist like Marcus, she was wondering if I could water her plants, and bring in her mail, I'd be welcome to stay as well, Daniel would be in Montreal all summer so the house would be empty, and I'd always seemed so at home here, she said, smiling, as the sun poured in through the window behind her and lined the edges of her face, her features darkened but their edges limned—and then she stood, left a hand on my shoulder as she moved towards the kitchen, saying, Well, you can think about it, you don't have to tell me now.

That night, after Ava had been put to bed and Phil had plodded up the stairs, I sought out Audrey in the kitchen, I found her doing the dishes, her shoulders hunched, her vertebrae visible, and asked her what she thought of it all, and she turned and paused for a moment, an illegible expression on her face, her mouth flat and closed. Let's take a walk, she said, and dried her hands and grabbed a jacket, and then we were outside, walking quickly down the sidewalk, Audrey's hands stuffed in her pockets and her head shot forward on her neck. She said that the first thing I should know is that anyone in Monique's position would have made the same choice, it wasn't really even a choice, there was no choice to make. When someone like Marcus Lyman asks you to work with him, she said, you simply don't turn him down, it would be crazy to turn him down. It would be suicide. You might as well stab yourself in the neck. Her eyes seemed to be scanning for something on the sidewalk, hunting something down, and I felt relieved, incredibly relieved not to be in her car, not to be driving with her, there was something extra in her, an energy more pressurized, more contained, and more explosive because contained. You have to understand how powerful he is, she said. It's a huge thing, a gigantic thing for Monique to be co-directing one of his plays, just having her name associated with him is huge, it could open so many doors for her, in fact it already has. She stopped, and turned towards me, the veins in her temples beating. The truth is, she said, there's no other way, at least not now, in this country, under this administration, there's no other way to survive. She put her hands back in her pockets and kept walking. Monique had to do this, she said. There's nothing else she could have done.

Lying in bed that night, I thought of the times I'd seen Marcus, I remembered the way he sat, his legs crossed, his fingers pressed together and pulsing, and in my mind I saw him sitting in a chair at the end of a long narrow street, and Monique was walking down the street, her footsteps echoing sharply, her hair blowing sideways in the wind, and I wanted to whisper in her ear, I wanted to be inside her ear whispering *don't do it.*

—

And so, twice a week, after work, I went to Monique's to water her plants, and bring in her mail, and do other small things she hadn't asked me to do, I swept her floors, wiped down her counters, and made sure her furniture hadn't moved, and opened the door of her refrigerator, peered inside, and closed it again, and straightened the tassels on her oriental rugs, and sorted the junk mail into one stack, the theater mail into another, and her personal letters into a third. I dusted her bookshelves. I shook the dirt from her doormat, organized the spices in her spice cabinet, and made a kind of floral arrangement of her spatulas and wooden spoons. I remembered reading somewhere that stars were only ever postponing their inevitable collapse, that they did this by burning the fuel of themselves, fusing the particles inside themselves, turning their innards into ovens. So I swept and dusted in a frenzy that kept my body burning all the time, and tried to hold in the front of my mind the thought that Monique had entrusted me with her house. And now I was here and she was not. And maybe it was because I was working too much and not eating enough, or maybe at the bookstore I'd inhaled too much dust, but in any case I started feeling dizzy and weak in the knees, like my body even with its burning wasn't enough, had already burned out or burned up. I sat down on the couch, pressed my fingers into my temples. A hoarse ruined voice was whispering in my ear, *hey Esther, hey Esther it's me, it's me Esther the Dead*. And then my vision wrinkled for a second, like a glitch in a film, and I saw myself sitting in the room where the light was always on. The bottom drawer of the dresser was open, and I was rising from my bed, reaching for the switch, and as I watched myself do this I thought, I've done this before, I've reached for this switch so many times, turned off this light a million times, and I'll have to keep turning it off for all eternity.

I stood up. I found myself staring down the long narrow hall, where the light that suffused the rest of the house didn't reach. Daniel's room lay at the end of that hall. I imagined a television set on his desk, where *Rat Trap* would be replaying endlessly, our faces growing more distorted each time, less like our faces each time. And I wanted to barge into that room, pull the tape from the mouth of the machine, and rip out its celluloid guts. But when I opened the door all I saw was a room from which every trace of Daniel had been removed. I looked in the closet, I opened drawers, I even peeked under the bed. He'd taken everything out, even the clothes he'd outgrown, the dice he used to use to play D&D. It was like he'd never lived there at all.

—

And then one day I stopped by the theater, having heard from Audrey that Monique had rented it out to a production company while she was gone. I slipped in through the backstage door, and walked through the warren of halls, surprised by the swarm of activity, people buzzing past me, their hair sculpted and lacquered, folders tucked under their arms. No one looked at me or even seemed to see me. I could have wandered those halls for thousands of years without ever being noticed. People were lined up outside some of the doors, studying themselves in pocket mirrors, applying makeup, memorizing lines, their lips moving without making sounds. I went into the theater, which had been turned into a film set, all blank reflective screens and bright lights, men milling about with clipboards. From an inconspicuous seat in the back I watched a woman stand in front of a round white screen, in a red dress, smiling, just trying to hold a smile, her teeth so white they looked radioactive, while three separate cameras honed in on her. I didn't understand why she had to hold her smile for so long, it looked painful, like someone had wedged a different mouth into her mouth. Then Antoine slid into the seat next to me, startling me until I saw it was him. Hey, he said. Hey, I said. What are you doing here? he said. I just stopped by, I said. I was curious. What are *you* doing here? He laughed without really laughing and said, I'm working. Oh, right, I said. There was a silence. We both looked back at the stage. What is this, anyways? I said. It's an ad, he said. The woman in red was still smiling her interminable smile. For what? I said. Antoine paused. He nodded and lifted his brows. Chicken, he said.

—

On our walk around the neighborhood, Paul pointed out all the places he'd worked, a couple bars, a barbershop, a flower shop, a fancy restaurant where he'd been the maître d, and he popped into these places and said hello to the people he knew, and said to be sure to send his love to this person or that, like he was sprinkling little bits of himself around the neighborhood, distributing himself through his network of acquaintances and friends. Often he stopped in front of a storefront and tried to remember what used to be there. He said that when you lived in a city for a long time you started to feel like everything used to be something else, as if the former things had left little traces of themselves, little itches in the depths of your memory. We walked down Broadway, past Dick's, the burger place, which had always been there, past the community college. We took a right on Pine and walked by the Egyptian, and then we circled around, came back up Olive. I asked Paul if he thought *he'd* still be here in a few years, not as in still alive, I corrected quickly, I meant still in Seattle, in this neighborhood. Who knows? he said, laughing. We were walking up through the residential streets, past the brick apartment buildings I loved, where I'd often dreamed of living, in a corner apartment on one of those upper floors, with a view of downtown, with a whole bestiary of books and records, with hardwood floors that would store enough light from the long summer days to keep the apartment glowing all winter. Of course, said Paul, at my age, it's tempting to think of this as the last chapter of my life. But then again, whenever I hear myself saying that, it's like a little moment of déjà vu. I've said the same thing so many times! We turned left on 11th, with its squat, crotchety houses, the vegetation in their yards overgrown, their porches tilting, then climbed the stairs to his house. It was brilliant at that hour, golden trapezoids aglow on the floor, Evelyn peeping short bright notes from her perch, everything motionless and shimmering. Paul brought in some iced tea, sat next to me on the couch, and asked for all my news, whatever I felt like sharing. I told him that Monique had gone to New York, and that since then things had felt less real for me. I told him that part of me was just waiting for her to return, to reopen the theater, to start working with the company again, but of course I had no idea if that would actually happen. But I said that I liked working with Audrey a lot, she was teaching me so many things, though I wasn't sure I could live with her much longer. Her house was a hard place to live, I said. Paul listened to all of this with a face like an open door, the corners of his eyes like hinges. And then he sighed. Well, I do have the room, he said slowly, looking at me with a measuring gaze. Kevin left? I said. He paused, and then, his voice lifting into a slightly higher register, he said, Yes, yes he did. And then he rose and led me into the room, which looked exactly as it did when I'd first moved in, just a bed and a desk, the one little window, sunlight filtering through the maple leaves, though now, on the wall, two photographs hung instead of one.

—

It was windy on the night Inez decided we all had to walk down the Pier, a warm evening wind that seemed to carry the whole summer inside it, all those long afternoons, the city breathing its aimless dreams in the heat, and all those twilight hours, when the sky recombined its colors, inventing new tints and hues, new notions of what a sky could be. The planet was hanging on the horizon, that red-orange eye whose name we didn't know, which nameless became our own planet, the planet that had come here for us, to protect us, destroy us, or just watch on idly as we protected or destroyed ourselves. There were ten or twelve of us, all drunk on beer or wine or whatever vile concoction we could drum up, and Stef had gone around slipping us some kind of pill, something nice he said, really nice, and Inez had seized on our suggestible states and convinced us to line both sides of the Pier, to form a kind of gauntlet, so that each of us could walk, do our little runway routine—just walk to the end of the Pier, turn around, and walk back. And I was there, watching everyone walk, watching Stef do his shambling mellow guy walk, all languid and loose-limbed, watching Maeve tuck her chin down dove-like into her neck, watching Inez lower her brow, lift her eyes, and bore her tunnel through to the future, until suddenly I wasn't—I'd slid back, been pulled back into the past, and was walking through the forest of doors, opening the door to the audition room, standing in the mud beneath the Pier. I was lying on the bed where a dead man had slept. Paul was saying, *but of course we're all going to die!* and I was slipping my arm into the silky sleeve of my black dinner jacket, and sweeping the stage, I could feel the rhythm of the broom, and Audrey was driving like a fury through the streets. I was drunk, the sky was changing colors, I was in the room where the light was always on, and the undead voice of Esther the Dead was whispering in my ear. Monique was giving me the key, the opera was soaring in Paul's house, and Daniel was training the eye of his camera on me, trapping me in his rat trap, and all of this was happening at the same time, I was living inside all these moments at once. And then I heard Inez saying, *Esther, Esther,* and I opened my eyes, saw that everyone was looking at me, telling me it was my turn to walk. Somehow I knew exactly what I wanted to do. I summoned Esther the Dead, I drew her up into my body, all her dead weight, her dead ends, and walked her off the end of the Pier.

ACKNOWLEDGEMENTS

I'd like to thank the editors at the literary journals where a few of these stories were originally published: "How We Got Into This" and "Moving Out" in *Conjunctions*, "What Was Left" in *Fence*, and "The Sky at Night" in *Ninth Letter*.

Thank you Andrew and Sam for bringing this book into the world with such thoughtfulness and care. Thanks Mike Corrao for the design work.

The play described in "Black Box" was loosely inspired by The Collected Works' 2013 San Francisco production of Witold Gombrowicz's *Princess Ivona*, directed by Michael Hunter, and starring Tonyanna Borkovi. My gratitude to the whole cast and crew of the play.

And a big warm thank you to all of you who have been my readers and literary interlocutors over the years.

AUTHOR BIO

Michael Holt is the author of the novella *The Seaside Hotel* (Sublunary Editions). His fiction has appeared in *Conjunctions, Fence, Gulf Coast, Ninth Letter,* and *The Threepenny Review,* among other journals. He grew up in Seattle, and currently resides in San Francisco. You can learn more about him at michaelwholt.com.

11:11 Press is an American independent literary publisher based in Minneapolis, MN. Founded in 2018, 11:11 publishes innovative literature of all forms and varieties. We believe in the freedom of artistic expression, the realization of creative potential, and the transcendental power of stories.

Milton Keynes UK
Ingram Content Group UK Ltd.
UKHW040834141024
449705UK00006B/240